Cowgirls

STORIES OF TRICK RIDERS, SHARP SHOOTERS, AND UNTAMED WOMEN

Edited by Erin Turner

TWODOT

GUILFORD, CONNECTICUT
HELENA, MONTANA
AN IMPRINT OF THE GLOBE PEQUOT PRESS

A · TWODOT® · BOOK

Copyright © 2009 by Morris Book Publishing, LLC

Text contributions by Greta Anderson, L. E. Bragg, Wynne Brown, Gayle C. Shirley, Beverly West

TwoDot is a registered trademark of Morris Book Publishing, LLC.

Text design by Sheryl P. Kober
Layout by Nancy Freeborn

Library of Congress Cataloging-in-Publication Data is available on file.
ISBN 978-0-7627-5535-6

Printed in the United States of America
10 9 8 7 6 5 4 3 2 1

CONTENTS

INTRODUCTION

The strong-willed, hard working, capable woman of the old West—the cowgirls—who could do a man's job better than a man, is an American icon that seems to most people a topic more of fiction than real fact. But the capable women of action who helped settle the West and did not live their lives by the Puritan standards that had been the norm for centuries for most women, were real live characters on the American frontier. These are women who helped to build this nation through their sacrifices, hard work, and the examples they set for others. They came to the West from diverse backgrounds and reacted to the new world in which they found themselves in many different ways. Most fron-

tierswomen found the experience liberating and energizing, despite its toughness and privations. Most brought a civilizing force in the communities in which they came to live. The stories in this book about American cowgirls reflect the can-do attitude that made America what it is today.

"Little Joe" Monaghan

Jo Monaghan
(1848–1904)

Cowboy Joe

The well-groomed mare trotted into town guided by her slight-statured rider. "Just another Eastern tenderfoot," noted the weather-worn prospectors and dusty cowpokes lining the sides of the crude main street. It was curious that this newcomer didn't carry a gun in this Wild West ruled by Colt and Winchester. Owyhee County's Ruby City was the center of Idaho's latest gold rush in 1867. Hopeful prospectors arrived every day, but there was something different about this one.

Standing barely 5 feet tall in his cowboy boots, wearing a baggy shirt, pants, and coat, this boy with the refined features and high-pitched voice would surely never last through the winter. Asked his name, the boy replied, "Joe Monaghan." It was not long before he was called nothing but Little Joe, due to the impression made by his appearance.

Little Joe purchased a pick and shovel in order to work the claim he had staked. The labor was grueling even for the most rugged of men, and Little Joe's hands were soon so blistered and bloodied he could barely continue working his claim. After giving up on prospecting, he took odd jobs and worked in the local mill; but whatever Little Joe did, he worked hard at it and won the respect of his tough neighbors.

Living in a rude Ruby City shack for more than ten years, Joe raised chickens and hogs. He made some money by keeping a cow and selling milk to the miners. Unlike the other men in town, Little Joe shied away from the saloons and card rooms, caring nothing for drink or dance-hall girls.

Feeling hemmed in by civilization, Little Joe took a job as a sheepherder and spent three years in this solitary occupation. With nothing but his horse and dog as companions, he tended his flock and fended off wolves through the long, snowy winters. After that Little Joe drifted between jobs, often working on cattle drives or wrangling and shearing sheep for local ranchers. Those he worked for described how the quiet cowboy never bathed or bunked with the other hands, preferring to lay out his bedroll under the stars alone.

Little Joe's only close friend was an older mine superintendent with whom he entrusted his hard-earned money for safekeeping. When Joe returned from cattle drives, he spent many an evening sitting on the porch of the superintendent's home shooting the breeze. It was a shock to everyone in town when the superintendent disappeared one day with Joe's life savings. The townsfolk, including Little Joe, formed a posse and chased after the thief, but nothing was ever seen of Joe's former friend or money.

A natural on horseback, Joe took to breaking wild broncs for a living. He became known throughout the Owyhees as a superior horseman. The *Idaho Capitol News* reported:

> *No horse was too wild or savage that he could not be brought to saddle and bit under Little Joe's hands. To this day the countryside about Silver City and Ruby City tell of his remarkable ability in this line. Many a campfire is brightened by the stories of the little horseman and his prowess in subduing untamed steeds of the range.*

A byproduct of riding the range was learning to shoot. Joe bought a six-shooter and practiced target shooting to try to develop his skill. Upon his return from one cattle drive, the locals noticed a marked improvement in Little Joe's shooting ability, as "he hit a can thrown in the air four out of five times, and was quick on the drop." Joe would say only that "some fellows from Texas" had been kind enough to show him a few tricks.

In the early 1880s Little Joe moved to Rockville and staked out a homestead claim about 10 miles west of town on Succor Creek along the Idaho/Oregon border. The foundation of Joe's log cabin was dug into the hillside, the low roof was covered in sod, and roughly hewn planks served as the door. His bed was a crude mattress filled with hay, which he shared with his horse during some sparse winters.

Little Joe loved the tiny town of Rockville, Idaho, with its population of twenty-one citizens. A civic-minded person, he voted in every election and served on several county-court juries.

Jo Monaghan debutante

Although a bit withdrawn, Little Joe greeted his neighbors as they rode past his ranch and was well liked by all.

Before long Joe had dozens of head in his own herd of cattle and horses. One old-timer reported to the *Rocky Mountain News*, "He was a familiar sight along the banks of Succor Creek with his band of buckskin horses all branded with the familiar 'J.M.'" The 1898 Rockville directory lists one "Joseph Monaghan, Cattleman."

Whether for companionship or money, Joe continued to take jobs on other ranches. He was a familiar sight in the sheep corrals at shearing time, driving cattle, or breaking horses for his neighbors. During the spring sheep shearing of 1897, Joe was wrangling on the Otto Albert ranch near Payette. Otto and his neighboring sheep ranchers knew of Joe's skill breaking wild broncs and suggested that he ought to try out for a Wild West show. The ranchers arranged a meeting between Little Joe and Andrew Whaylen, a former member of Buffalo Bill's Wild West Show who was starting his own company.

Any misgivings he might have had must have been alleviated when Joe met Whaylen on the train platform in Iowa. Andrew Whaylen, dressed in a fringed buckskin coat, was no taller than Joe himself. Andy advertised his show on the sides of three painted wagons he owned: WHAYLEN'S WILD WEST SHOW. THE GREATEST SHOW ON LAND OR SEA. Whaylen's Wild West Show featured Cowboy Joe, and $25 was offered to any man who could bring in a bronc that Joe couldn't ride. Little Joe was able to ride any bucking horse with ease, even horses that had thrown all the local riders.

Always the showman, Whaylen read a newspaper article about the Vitagraph Film Company that touted the moving picture as the coming thing. Whaylen wrote to the film company and suggested they film his show. Albert Smith of the Vitagraph Film Company was eager to accept the invitation, stating that this would be the first Western movie to be filmed west of the Mississippi. The show's star performer, Cowboy Joe Monaghan, was filmed on a bucking bronc, earning him a spot in film history.

Little Joe seemed uncomfortable with the spotlight, and when the Wild West Show closed for the season, he took the train back to his ranch near Rockville. Although Whaylen urged him to return to the show the next year, Joe refused, preferring to spend his time quietly at his ranch. His only companion on the ranch was a Chinese cook he hired to help around the homestead. When the old cook died, Little Joe appeared to shut himself away more than ever.

In late 1903 Joe was driving his cattle to winter pasture on the Boise River when he took ill. He was taken to the Malloy ranch for nursing, and the Malloy boys drove the cattle on to the river. Mrs. Malloy tended to Little Joe the best she could, but he had developed pneumonia, and in the first week of January 1904, Little Joe Monaghan lost his life amid a coughing fit.

Word of Little Joe's death spread throughout the valley, and neighboring ranchers came to the Malloys to tend to the body and build a coffin for their friend. The ranchers never could have imagined what they would find when they attempted to dress the body of this man who had voted, served on juries, and was the first western cowboy to appear in the movies. They found that Little Joe was really Little "Jo," a woman.

The tale of this woman who had spent nearly forty years living on the range as a cowboy not only stunned the local community but became national news. When the story was printed in Kansas, it was theorized that Jo may have been Kate Bender—"Kansas City Kate"—a saloon dancer who had murdered two people and fled Kansas, never to be seen again. Although headlines promoting this theory popped up in Idaho, those who knew Jo dismissed the idea.

Two plausible theories on Jo Monaghan's identity emerged from the rumors. The first centered around a neighbor remembering that he

WHEN THINGS DO NOT GO RIGHT WITH YOU, WHEN THE CIRCUMSTANCES SEEM TO BE AGAINST YOU AND FATE DEALS YOU A BLOW BETWEEN THE EYES, REMEMBER WHAT THE COWBOYS SAY IN THE GREAT NORTHWEST. "JUST GRIT YOUR TEETH, GET ANOTHER HOLD AND LET 'ER BUCK!"

—The motto of the Pendleton Roundup, 1911

had mailed letters for Jo to a Walters family in Buffalo, New York. He wrote to the chief of police in Buffalo to determine whether Jo had left any heirs. Police Matron Anna Walters received the letter and responded. A Johanna Monaghan had been adopted by Miss Walters's mother. Johanna's mother had died when she was eight years old, and the stepfather left to raise the girl mistreated her terribly. At the age of fourteen, Johanna took her departure, telling the Walterses that she was going west to make her fortune. The Walters family received frequent letters from Johanna describing her work in mining camps and on ranches. Though she never told the Walterses she was living as a man, when Mrs. Walters asked for a picture of Jo, she was sent a head shot of Jo with very short hair, wearing a man's suit. Anna Walters even produced the photograph of a very masculine-looking Jo. This photo was printed in a Buffalo newspaper with the caption "Buffalo Woman Who Masqueraded for Years As a Cowboy Out West."

Another story evolved when neighboring ranchers went through Jo's possessions after her death. The ranchers found photographs and letters between Jo and her sister in Buffalo, New York. The letters told the story of a Buffalo debutante who had been disowned by her wealthy family for giving birth out of wedlock to a son, Laddie.

One such letter, dated September 11, 1868, was addressed to Josephine Monaghan, Rockville, Idaho:

Dear Sister,

I have lain awake nights picturing you in your wild wanderings and with your boy pressed tightly in my arms I have prayed to a merciful God to keep you safe and unharmed.

When I think of all my comforts and luxuries and then of my Josephine sleeping by night on a blanket and traveling by day with that crowd of rough men and uncouth women you describe in your letter I feel I cannot bear it.

I am glad you have decided to stay in one place, although the camp sounds so awful. Still, I know where to find you.

Laddie is sitting on the floor beside me. He had a slight cold last week but is quite well now. I hardly know how to live without him. I also am well and still longing for your return. It takes so long

> for a letter to reach me that I hope you will not delay in answering this one.
>   Your last letter was such a comfort. Goodbye now and with lots of love from Laddie and Helen

The series of letters painted a picture of a desperate single mother trying to carve out a living by working as a waitress at a restaurant on Broadway in New York City. Her son was born in 1866, and Jo had been abandoned by the baby's father. She had been forced, for a time, to put the baby into an asylum. When all of this became too much for the young mother, she placed the boy in the care of her younger sister and set out for the West.

It seemed from the tone of the correspondence that the child had been told his mother was dead. A later letter from Helen informed Jo of Laddie's graduation from Columbia Law School and subsequent admission to the New York State Bar Association.

There, among the faded letters that told the story of Jo Monaghan's evolution from society debutante to Idaho cowboy, was an old daguerreotype of a lovely young woman making her society debut. Who could have guessed, upon the occasion of her "coming out" in society, that this beautiful, teenaged debutante would die a lonely Idaho rancher at the age of fifty-six?

Jo Monaghan's final resting place is a community cemetery on the Hat H ranch near her beloved Rockville. Her true identity may never be known.

When a cowgirl dies and goes to Heaven she does not get a halo.
Instead she gets a big silver belt buckle.

—Jill Charlotte Stanford

Kitty C. Wilkins

(1857–1936)

Queen of Diamonds

Nothing could have prepared the two young cowboys for their encounter with the approaching rider. A golden palomino galloped up the dusty ranch-house road that late summer day. The horse's flowing yellow mane and tail were a perfect match for the rider's own flaxen mane. The startled cowboys stared in disbelief at the stunningly beautiful blue-eyed blonde coming toward them. After riding for several days along the border between Idaho and Nevada in search of work with a cattle outfit, the gorgeous woman before them seemed like an apparition.

Regaining his composure, the younger of the two asked, "Can you tell us where we can find the boss?"

"I am the boss," replied the woman firmly.

The two youthful cowboys had just met the legendary "Horse Queen of Idaho," Kitty Wilkins. Through her talent for raising and trading horses and penchant for garnering publicity, Kitty also earned titles such as "The Golden Queen" and "The Queen of Diamonds." The latter was a reference to her ownership of the Diamond Ranch.

The daughter of two western pioneers, J. R. and Laura K. Wilkins, Kitty was born in Jacksonville, Oregon, in 1857. Twenty-one-year-old J. R. Wilkins and seventeen-year-old Laura were married in 1853 in Fort Madison, Iowa, where he had moved from Indiana and she from Maine. Shortly after their marriage, the Wilkins couple joined a wagon train to follow the Oregon Trail west. They resided in Oregon City and then in the Rogue River Valley at Jacksonville, where Kitty was born, before moving to California. A gold rush brought the family to Florence, Idaho, in 1862. Kitty took great pride in the fact that her mother was the first woman to arrive at the gold camp. She said, "I feel that my brother and I can justly claim that our parents came to Idaho before any others."

After making several more moves in and out of Idaho, J. R. Wilkins settled his wife and children on a large spread in southern Idaho's Bruneau Valley. The Wilkins Island Ranch was located on land at the fork of the Bruneau River near Jarbidge Mountain, rather than on an actual island. The Wilkinses' holdings spread to other outposts along the Snake River, at Mountain Home and into Nevada. Their range was 75 miles away from the main ranch, stretching into the Owyhee Mountains.

Although her father had several thousand head of cattle and horses, Kitty always preferred raising horses to cattle. In addition to loving horses, the shrewd Miss Wilkins saw them as much more profitable, stating, "A 3 or 4 year-old steer. . . worth but $20, while a horse of the same age is worth $85–$100. . . . horses are much more easily raised and do not require half the care."

Considering it romantic, Kitty loved to tell reporters about her start in the business. Neighbors bidding the Wilkins family goodbye upon one of their departures from Oregon gave two-year-old Kitty two $20 gold pieces. Her father bought the toddler a filly, and, as Kitty put it, "from the increase all of my bands have come."

Kitty was a gifted rider whose brothers taught her to shoot both pistols and rifles proficiently, "that being a necessary part of a woman's education out there [in the West] in those days." Kitty was sent to a private school for girls in San Jose, California, for her formal education and social refinement. She also traveled throughout the United States to all the major cities as part of her cultural enlightenment.

Upon returning to Idaho she was at first lonely, until she developed a taste for the family horse business. Kitty later expressed her feelings about Idaho and her business to an Eastern reporter, "Do I like living away out in Idaho? Oh, so much! I go out to roundups in the spring and fall and enjoy myself ever so much. It is a fascinating business and grows upon you."

When her father took young Kitty on one of his trips east to a horse market, she became hooked on the business of selling horses. From that time on she constantly accompanied her father to market his horses. Within a few years of that first trip, Kitty had developed her own distinct marketing plan and could sell horses better than her father. She was a shrewd businesswoman and an excellent judge of horseflesh. She prided herself on selling only high-quality stock. To one Midwestern reporter she boasted, "I bring the best stock to market that comes from the West. I never ship a blemished animal from the ranch. They are all sound when they leave there."

Kitty and her younger brothers eventually took over their father's ranch. While her brothers concentrated on cattle ranching, Kitty took

Kitty C. Wilkins

COWGIRL IS AN ATTITUDE, REALLY. A PIONEER SPIRIT, A SPECIAL AMERICAN BRAND OF COURAGE. THE COWGIRL FACES LIFE HEAD ON, LIVES BY HER OWN LIGHTS, AND MAKES NO EXCUSES. COWGIRLS TAKE STANDS. THEY SPEAK UP. THEY DEFEND THE THINGS THEY HOLD DEAR. A COWGIRL MIGHT BE A RANCHER, OR A BARREL RACER, OR A BULL RIDER, OR AN ACTRESS. BUT SHE'S JUST AS LIKELY TO BE A CHECKER AT THE LOCAL WINN DIXIE, A FULL-TIME MOTHER, A BANKER, AN ATTORNEY, OR AN ASTRONAUT."

—Dale Evans, "The Queen of the Cowgirls," 1992

over the horse outfit. No one ever questioned Kitty's authority or business sense. She was the undisputed boss of the Diamond Ranch.

Wild horses abounded on the range between Nevada's Humboldt River and Idaho's Snake River. These mustangs became the property of anyone who could catch and put a brand on them. Kitty saw a way to expand her own small herd, started with the purchase of the $40 filly when she was just two. She hired the best riders and set out to claim every unbranded mustang from the Nevada/Idaho line to the Owyhee River in Oregon. Kitty registered the Diamond Brand, a brand that was to become synonymous with fine horse stock, and set to work branding every wild horse she could bring in.

In addition to registering her own brand, hiring the finest cowboys available, and raising sound stock, Kitty marketed her horses in the most lucrative fashion. She bought stallions from around the world to develop her stock. Her lines included Clydesdales, Percherons, Morgans, Normans, and Hambletonians. After this she claimed to have "no native Oregon or Spanish horses" on her ranch.

Rumors put the Diamond Ranch holdings at 20,000 head of horses. In reality that number may have been closer to 5,000 head on the ranch at any one time. It took up to forty men during fall roundup to cut out and brand stock on the Diamond Ranch.

Kitty's marketing skills got her contracts with lucrative horse markets in the East and as far away as Dawson City in the Yukon Territory. One of her best customers was the United States Cavalry. At one point she was supplying six train cars of broke horses every two weeks to Eastern markets. Since each stock car held twenty-six horses, Kitty's hands had to break 156 horses for each shipment. Because the Diamond Ranch cowboys were breaking broncs continuously, they became known throughout the West as some of the West's most skilled riders.

Kitty Wilkins ran the "hardest riding outfit west of the Mississippi River," according to Harvey St. John, Kitty's youngest bronc rider and personal friend. Cowboys who rode with the Diamond Ranch were among the finest in the world. Buffalo Bill's Wild West Show hired some of the Wilkinses' horsemen; others became top rodeo champions. The young cowboy described riding for Kitty: "If a man weren't a good rider when he went to work for her, he was a good rider when he left or he wasn't riding at all—unless in a hearse."

The Queen of Diamonds ruled her cowboys with an iron hand. Although they were hard-edged, rough-hewn characters, some of whom became notorious outlaws, they respected Kitty, and her word was law on the Diamond Range. Any hand that disobeyed her was run off the range immediately.

The lovely horse queen caused an instant sensation when she arrived in the East to market her animals. As her obituary characterized it: "The sight of a beautiful, slender, young blonde, dressed in modish fashion, personally selling her stock, and knowing a complete knowledge of each horse's good points, created a furore [sic]." Citizens of the Eastern cities were awed by Kitty Wilkins's beauty and grace. She was interviewed wherever her travels took her. A reporter in St. Louis was stunned by Kitty's looks and so described their meeting:

> *The reporter was hardly prepared to meet the tall young woman, dressed in a swell, tailor-made costume, her blonde curls surmounted by a dainty Parisian creation, who greeted him with perfect self-possession. One might be excused for imagining that Western ranch life would coarsen any woman, no matter what her natural tendencies might be, but one glimpse of Miss Wilkins is enough to completely dissipate the idea. She is a strikingly attractive woman.*

Meanwhile, a Sioux City reporter described Kitty as a

> *. . . tall stately blonde, with fluffy, golden hair, large blue eyes that have quite a knack of looking clear through one, regular features and pearly teeth which glisten and sparkle when she smiles, and she has a habit of smiling very frequently. Her lips are red and full, and her mouth and chin denote a certain firmness of manner, no doubt acquired in her peculiar calling.*

San Francisco awarded Kitty their "Palm" for beauty when she visited that city. This was an honor bestowed by the local newspapers and reported in the society pages.

Being the most notable, if not only, woman horse dealer in the country, Kitty attracted a great deal of attention from the press. She was adept at public relations, promoting her fame wherever she went.

The beautiful Kitty never married. It is said that she loved only one man in her life— the Diamond Ranch's top foreman. He and Kitty were engaged to be married when the engagement ended violently. Kitty's fiancé was shot in a typical range dispute over a watering hole. Reportedly Kitty never showed a romantic interest in another man.

The end of World War I also signaled the end to prosperity in the horse market. Automobiles and machinery were taking the place of horses. Irrigation projects took over the once-expansive horse ranges.

Kitty saw the changes occurring and, already a wealthy woman, decided to retire from the business. She chose to spend her remaining years in a grand home in Glenns Ferry. People who knew Kitty claimed that her beauty never really faded. Even in retirement she kept abreast of current issues and progress across America.

A respected Idaho pioneer, Kitty was a guest of honor at the Boise Centennial Celebration. She headed the pioneer parade in a horse-drawn carriage. The horse queen's ornate saddle was put on display at the Idaho State Historical Museum, along with her portrait.

Kitty C. Wilkins died of a heart attack at the age of seventy-nine on October 8, 1936, at her home in Glenns Ferry, and was buried in Mountain Home.

Perhaps the passing of this notable pioneer horsewoman can best be described in Kitty's own words. When her brother and business partner, John, passed away just three weeks prior to her own death, Kitty reflected:

The years are taking their toll of these early pioneers and few remain to tell us of the romantic beginning of the wonderful west we know. It is difficult for us, in our ease and comfort of present day surroundings, to conceive of the hardships, the privations and the suffering endured by these men and women that they might establish and build up a country for their families and those who would follow.

OF COURSE, IT'S ALWAYS THE SAME THING, I GET CHASED, ABUSED, NEARLY KILLED, RESCUED IN THE NICK OF TIME, LOVED, HATED—AND FINALLY THERE'S A HAPPY FOREVER AFTER!

— Marie Wiescamp, 1919, star of dozens of Western serial movies.

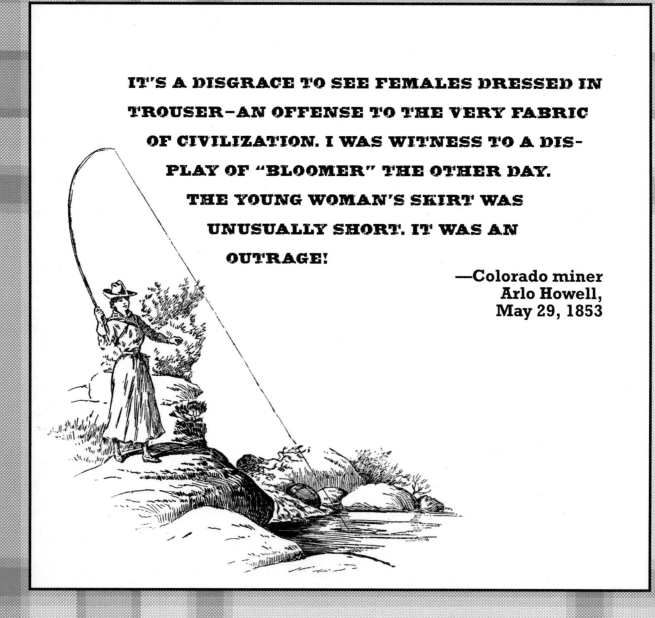

IT'S A DISGRACE TO SEE FEMALES DRESSED IN TROUSER—AN OFFENSE TO THE VERY FABRIC OF CIVILIZATION. I WAS WITNESS TO A DISPLAY OF "BLOOMER" THE OTHER DAY. THE YOUNG WOMAN'S SKIRT WAS UNUSUALLY SHORT. IT WAS AN OUTRAGE!

—Colorado miner
Arlo Howell,
May 29, 1853

Alice Day Pratt

(1872-1963)

Dry-Land Homesteader

Alice Day Pratt shivered inside her canvas tent as the slate-gray sky spit snowflakes the size of dimes. For more than a month, temperatures had hovered near zero at her marginal homestead in central Oregon. Her supply of firewood was perilously low, and she could hardly find even slivers of juniper under the deepening snow.

Desperate for warmth, Alice split into kindling her large chopping block, the last relic of a wagonload of firewood that friends had delivered several months ago. It flared into a welcome blaze, but the comforting heat didn't last long.

Years later, she recalled her growing desperation as she struggled to survive single-handedly: "On the next day—the blizzard continuing—I burned my ladder, and on the next would have sacrificed my steps, had not a blessed chinook blown up in the night, carried the snow away in foaming torrents, and laid bare many a rich and unsuspected treasure of fuel."

The serendipitous chinook wind helped Alice to endure that grueling winter of 1913, but at least as significant were her own hard work, grit, and resourcefulness. She summoned those traits time and time again as she tried to tame an unforgiving land, or at least to reach some kind of compromise with it. Although she eventually had to abandon her "homesteading dream," she managed to outlast many a fellow dreamer.

Later in life, Alice looked back on her homestead years with mixed feelings:

I have known lean years and leaner years, hope and discouragement, good fortune and disaster, friendship and malice, righteousness, generosity, and double dealing. . . . Now and then I have known burdens—most often physical burdens—too heavy for mortals to bear. I have been cold and hungry and ragged and penniless. I have been free and strong and buoyant and glad.

Alice Day Pratt was part of the last wave of homesteaders who flooded the West in the early twentieth century—spurred on by passage of the Enlarged Homestead Act of 1909. Earlier emigrants to Oregon had already snatched most of the moist and fertile acreage in the western part of the state, so the latecomers had to settle for vast expanses of semiarid uplands east of the Cascades.

The new homesteaders often were unaware of how unforgiving and unprofitable this dry land could be. Pamphlets published by the railroads and other promoters had convinced them that the land was fecund and plentiful, just waiting to reward with riches those who got there first. The homesteaders also believed that the West offered adventure and independence. Here was one last chance to grab a piece of the quintessential American dream.

Alice herself had imagined being "afar on the prairies with the wind in my hair and the smell of new-plowed earth in every breath I drew." By heading west, she expected to put behind her a life of competition, high pressure, and "extremes of gayety [sic] and misery." Ahead, she envisioned hope, freedom, opportunity, and limitless spaces.

While Alice shared the same dreams and hopes of many homesteaders, she differed from most of them in an obvious way: She was a single woman in what was predominantly a man's world. Of the tens of thousands of people who filed homestead claims in the early 1900s, only about ten to fifteen percent were unmarried women, according to some historians.

Alice was unique in yet another way. She was one of only a few women who left behind an extensive firsthand account of her homesteading experience. In her book, *A Homesteader's Portfolio,* published in 1922, she described how she moved to Oregon at the age of thirty-nine and "proved up" a homestead some sixty miles east of Bend. In engaging detail, she told of enduring drought and dust, hostile neighbors and hungry hawks, loneliness and larcenous rabbits. Although she presented the book as a work of fiction, the account is obviously autobiographical.

Author Molly Glass, in her introduction to the book, described it as "an especially significant work" because it presented "not only a rare but an extraordinarily complete report of the life of a single-handed woman homesteader on a landscape fraught with peril and difficulty—a woman not the victim of her circumstances but taking her place as a part of history, and a maker of history."

Over the years, Alice wrote other articles and books, including a self-published memoir,

Three Frontiers, which delved into her Minnesota childhood. She was born in June 1872 to William and Sophie Pratt at the family's cottage near Mankato. Her father, a native of Connecticut, thrived on adventure but wasn't particularly adept at business. When his lumber company began to fail in 1877, he set off for the Black Hills of South Dakota, hoping to establish a prosperous lumber business among the hordes of miners lured there by the discovery of gold. He left his young family behind and returned home only for brief visits. Not until 1886 was the family reunited on a remote homestead in Little Elk Canyon, fifteen miles north of Rapid City and twenty-five miles from William Pratt's business in Deadwood.

Alice's father continued to spend much of his time away from home, so many of the heavy chores fell to her. She helped care for two younger siblings and an ailing grandfather, toted heavy pails of water up a steep slope from a spring, tended the garden, looked after the horses, and trekked two miles to a small country store when the family needed supplies.

Alice's only schooling took place at home. She pored over books about plants and animals and hiked the Black Hills collecting specimens for her studies. Her interest in natural history became a lifelong pursuit. She wrote essays about flora and fauna for various magazines, and she published a children's book, *Animal Babies,* in 1941.

Although Alice's childhood in South Dakota was stark and demanding, she later would remember those years fondly. "We were always warm in the house and no fears beset us," she wrote. "Life was so simple that not much could happen to it."

Eventually, Alice left home to become a teacher. But, after working at schools in North Carolina and Arkansas, she pined for a more adventurous life. She began thinking seriously about her childhood desire to acquire her own "portion of the earth's crust" on the Western frontier. She had very little money and couldn't afford to buy land, but she knew she could get some free if she homesteaded. She decided to take a teaching job in northeastern Oregon where she could begin scouting for promising property.

Once in Oregon, Alice hired a "locator," who identified 160 acres in the middle of the state, near a tiny town called Post. As soon as Alice heard about the parcel in the fall of 1911, she dashed off to inspect it. She was smitten at first sight. Standing at the foot of Friar Butte amid sagebrush and junipers, she envisioned the butte as her upland pasture. The deep wash at its foot she saw planted in grain. Off in the distance, she spotted timbered mountains and a cleft cut by the Crooked River. She could see no houses or other signs of human habitation.

Alice knew she was home. She selected a handsome, cone-shaped juniper and decided it would stand in her dooryard. As she turned and looked over the sweeping valley, she picked a name for her homestead: Broadview.

Alice's first order of business was to file the proper papers at the local land office. Under the Enlarged Homestead Act, she got title to the land, but she couldn't sell or mortgage it until she had lived there and made improvements for three years.

Her second order of business was to return to northeastern Oregon to complete the school year and pack her belongings. She arrived back at her dry-land homestead on June 20, 1912, pitched a tent, and set to work. Homestead law required her to cultivate five of every forty acres within three years of taking possession. She had equipment to assemble, fields to plow, seed to buy, shelters to erect, firewood to collect, water to haul—so many chores they were nearly overwhelming.

Alice realized she would need help. When some of her new neighbors stopped by to say hello, she asked about the availability of hired hands. A few of the neighbors volunteered assistance, but rarely did they commit to a specific task and time. Once, neighbors offered to haul wood to help her construct a tent house, but they postponed the job week after week, even as fall approached.

Early one August, another neighbor agreed to plow forty acres so Alice could plant a wheat crop, but by mid-October the sod still lay undisturbed. Finally, the ground froze so hard it would no longer yield to the plow. An irate Alice later learned that the man had taken other jobs and had been leaving hers for last. As a result, she would have no wheat crop the following spring.

"My difficulties have been far oftener with the human element than with the rigors of the climate or the hardships of labor," she wrote in *A Homesteader's Portfolio*.

Alice had most of her problems with "Old Oregonians"—longtime ranchers who disdained the new homesteaders. One of them once bluntly told her, "The only way to deal with them homesteaders is to starve 'em out."

Fortunately, Alice also had a handful of good, caring, helpful friends, most of them newly arrived homesteaders like herself. With them, she enjoyed basket socials, dances, picnics, pageants, and other pleasant gatherings. These were welcome diversions from the physical and psychological hardships of her life.

Being a single woman, Alice occasionally found herself deflecting the advances of local bachelors. She feared "the life-long bond" of marriage, but, to her own surprise, she found some men appealing. After an evening walk with one young friend and neighbor, she confessed, "What sort of old maid am I anyway that I can't walk home in the moonlight with an attractive boy without tingling from head to foot! Good reason why devoted hermits segregate themselves. In the peace of Broadview I haven't felt this way for lo these many moons."

With few friends and neighbors on whom she could rely, Alice often turned to animal companions to help her combat the loneliness of her solitary life. She kept cats, horses, dogs, and chickens. The latter, she wrote, would "gather in little groups about me as I work here and there, engaging me in cheery conversation, essaying little familiarities and friendly overtures, even performing certain stunts with self-conscious gravity, delighting in personal attention."

Alice also felt a special attachment to her milk cow, Bossy, and Bossy's calf, Psalmmy. The calf resisted Alice's efforts to wean it, but she badly needed Bossy's milk for her own consumption and to earn extra income. When Alice confined Bossy to pasture, Psalmmy would follow Alice around the yard, suck the doorknob of her house, and roll his eyes to express his hunger. The calf was clever enough to circumvent Alice's many creative attempts to restrain him. When she tried muzzles, Psalmmy simply nuzzled them aside. When she smeared red-pepper paste on Bossy's teats, Psalmmy smacked his lips but then ignored the fiery sauce. When Alice built a fence to corral Bossy, Psalmmy found a gap. Years later, Alice described her frustrations.

I tried another fence. I tried another pasture. I tried the government reserve twenty miles distant. Always sundown of a day sooner or later arrived that brought Bossy and Psalmmy peacefully home together, Bossy released of her rich and ample load, Psalmmy rolling in his gait and stupid to inebriety. No wires were too closely set, no gate too high, no location too distant for the ingenuity or the valor of his ruling passion.

Neighbors counseled Alice to butcher Psalmmy, but she couldn't do it; she had become too attached to the clever calf. Instead, she finally erected a fence tall enough to complete the job of weaning.

Domestic critters were not Alice's only worries. She battled coyotes that harassed her stock, rabbits that munched her crops, and hawks that snatched her chickens. She scared away some of the hawks with well-timed shotgun blasts but failed to hit any. She tried poisoning the rabbits but had limited success.

In truth, Alice did not have the heart to try more lethal weapons. In her writings, she lamented the cruelty that was needed to keep the pests under control. She also worried about upsetting the balance of nature—a decidedly progressive sentiment for an early-twentieth-century homesteader. She wrote:

For a thousand years, presumably, this vast plateau which is now my home has been covered with sagebrush and bunch grass and sprinkled with juniper trees, and has supported a normal population of jack rabbits and sage rats. Then suddenly comes man with his alien stock, his dogs and his cats, his new and succulent crops, with their admixture of weed seeds and germs of insect life. And lo, this quiet and harmonious state of nature is all in turmoil.

Alice's own existence on her dry-land homestead was always tenuous. She spent several years living in a tent house, which would shake "like a rat" in storms and heat up like an oven on blistering summer days. It was cozy in the winter only if she had plenty of firewood.

Eventually, neighbors helped her to build a barn and a rickety twenty-by-twelve-foot wooden house. It had a single room with a kitchen and shelves at one end and a table, cot, and bookshelves at the other.

Alice could not afford a sturdier home or more household conveniences. She had to hoard her money for necessities, such as seeds and plowing. She sold chickens, eggs, alfalfa, hay, grain, and vegetables, but her earnings never amounted to much. At times, she had to take teaching jobs to make ends meet.

As soon as Alice proved up her homestead by meeting the residency requirement, she traveled to the East to visit her family and earn some money. She returned to Broadview two years later, in 1918, but funds were still short and she had to take another teaching job ten miles away at Conant Basin. It enabled her to cling to her "homesteading dream" despite the drought, bad weather, and poor commodity prices that had driven so many others off the land. In 1921, she wrote:

> Over my six hundred and forty acres—thus increased by a second beneficent allowance— roams a beautiful little Jersey herd. A group of dear white ponies call me mistress. White biddies still dot my hill slopes and cackle ceaselessly. Pax, an Armistice Day puppy, and El Dorado, son of Kitty Kat, have succeeded those earlier friends whose gentle spirits still wander with me on the sagebrush slopes. There is a mortgage. There is still necessity to teach. My little flock of orphan citizens still beckons from the future. Yet, for me, the wilderness and the solitary place have been glad, and nature has not betrayed the heart that loved her.

Alice held onto her homestead even as drought persisted into the 1920s. The good topsoil blew away, wells dried up, and the soil grew more alkaline. To make things worse, prices for grain and dairy products were dropping, and harsh winters battered the plains. The winter of 1924–1925 was ruthless. One day a blinding storm dumped enough snow to reach the upper sashes of the school where Alice was teaching. Two days later, temperatures plummeted to thirty-three degrees below zero—the lowest Alice had ever experienced. She had to kick her way through deep snow to check on her chickens. As she later recalled:

> Twenty young cocks, as white as the snow drifts, sat starkly upon their perches as if enchanted. There was a statuesqueness about them that sent a chill over me, cold as I was. No, they were not dead, but thos [sic] wattles that characterize their breed were as hard and stiff as plaster. Their feet were not frozen. It was the evening dip in the water that had done the mischief. Dabbling in the water had started the freezing before the night's cold had found them. Full-feeding was all that had saved the flock from death.

On her way back to her house, Alice was struck by its appearance, "lost in the wilderness of snow, and fringed with icicles almost to the ground." Later in her life, as she lay in bed in a comfortably warm apartment, she sometimes wondered if the little house still stood "in a wilderness of snow, and whether little calves are crying in the willows."

After that frigid winter, Alice enjoyed a few years of better weather, but it was not to last. Another drought struck in 1928. Alice was forced to take out a large loan, and a year later she had to sell her dairy herd to repay it. In 1930, she gave her chickens and horses to neighbors, shuttered her little house on the prairie, and climbed on the train for one last trip to the East. She must have held out hope of seeing Broadview again, because she didn't sell it until 1950.

Most dry-land settlers had packed up and fled long before Alice. By 1920, only half of the original homestead population remained. By 1940, two-thirds of the land allotted under the homestead act had reverted to the federal government.

After moving back to the East, Alice lived with her mother and her sister Marjorie, first in Niagara Falls and then in New York City. She continued to teach and write magazine articles and books. Some of her manuscripts were published, while others gathered dust on a shelf. Late in life, Alice suffered from crippling arthritis and was confined to her apartment, though her intellect and spirit remained strong to the end. Alice died on January 11, 1963, at the age of ninety.

Although, in the long run, Alice had not succeeded at homesteading, she had demonstrated the stamina and resourcefulness of women at a time when women's capabilities were underestimated. She had also learned a valuable lesson, which she summed up shortly after turning eighty:

Success may be the smallest and least important of the fruits of endeavor; it is the endeavor itself, the opportunity to use one's whole self completely—initiative, creativity, and physical strength—that is its own reward: and it may well be that one looks back upon the times of greatest strain and anxiety as the high points in [one's] pilgrimage.

Sarah Bowman

(1813–1866)

The Great Western

It was early in the year 1846. Zachary Taylor and one-thousand men were on a march southward from Corpus Christi. They were headed to defend the southern border of the newly annexed state of Texas and had trudged for more than two weeks. As the troops prepared to file down a steep embankment, a commotion of bugle cries broke out on the other shore. From the cloud of dust, a warning was delivered, "Cross this stream and you'll be shot!" The column of Americans came to a halt.

Suddenly a 6-foot-tall woman with blazing red hair appeared at the head of the line. Sarah Boujette had proven herself a handy laundress and cook in the Corpus Christi camp. Her husband, being sick, had taken the water route with the other sick and wounded—and the military wives—to the supply base at Point Isabel. But not Sarah: She wanted a piece of the action. Before the trek she had purchased a wagon and mule team to carry the pots and pans and army rations from which she made a daily "mess," and she traveled overland with the troops.

Now she was face-to-face with Zachary Taylor, one of her personal heroes. If truth be told, she was more than face-to-face; she had a solid 4-inch advantage over the stocky commander. She proclaimed loudly so that all could hear, "If the general would give me a strong pair of tongs, I'd wade that river and whip every scoundrel that dared show himself."

What did she mean by "a strong pair of tongs"? This blue-eyed colossus may have intended a couple of things. Metal tongs for grasping and serving food were certainly part of any mess cook's supply; one can imagine that a strong pair, properly wielded, could inflict some damage on the assailed. But there was more to it than that. Just a year before, a new style had become fashionable in men's work pants. These new pants were being called "tongs."

Sarah was ready to show the soldiers how to fight like men.

Electrified by her example and the language that she used, the men charged down the arroyo and up the other side unscathed. The Mexicans scattered, their bluff called. And the woman who had rallied the men past this first hurdle was soon nicknamed "The Great Western" after the first steamship to cross the Atlantic, eight years before. That afternoon she stood in the stream to help some of the less able travelers across. Sarah was ironclad, in personality and physique. And like a ship, she was most definitely a "she."

The Great Western was born in the wilds of Missouri in 1813—or was it Tennessee in 1817? Sarah changed the details each time the census taker came around. Either way, she was raised on the border between civilization and wilderness and had no formal schooling. Her business agreements and census interviews are never signed with more than an X. With a married name of Boujette, it's possible that her first husband, like many other Frenchmen in the West at that time, was involved in the fur trade.

Sarah's career with the army got off to a modest start in 1840. She claimed that she and her husband first served under Zachary Taylor in the Seminole War in Florida, though there are no stories of a big, bold, red-haired woman in first-hand accounts from that war. According to her they were recruited from Missouri by a captain named George Lincoln, who also followed Taylor to Mexico. Although there is no historical proof, her fierce demonstrations of loyalty to both Lincoln and Taylor in the Mexican War suggest that she knew them previously. Joining the Florida battle in her twenties would certainly have been in character; Sarah would follow the army her whole life long.

Shortly after the encounter with the Mexicans at the arroyo, Sarah's wagon arrived along with the rest of the overland troops at their destination near the mouth of the Rio Grande. The Mexican army had gathered across the river, in the town of Matamoros. During a month of uneasy peace, Sarah did laundry and cooked, as did a handful of other military wives. Meanwhile, Taylor erected a fort, later to be named Fort Brown.

One of Sarah's most famous stands came in the skirmishes that followed. The majority of the men had been sent to defend the supply post at Point Isabel, 20 miles away. Only five-hundred remained at Fort Brown to face the five-thousand Mexicans on the other shore. At five o'clock on the morning of May 3, 1846, the Mexicans began shelling the American fort. Most of the women immediately retreated to the bomb shelters to sew sandbags, but not Sarah. At seven o'clock she served breakfast in the fort's courtyard, sidestepping lit cannonballs as she stoked the cook fires, stirred the kettles, and served up black coffee.

The shelling continued around the clock for seven days. During that time Sarah carried buckets of coffee to the artillerymen stationed along the fort's walls and offered regular meals at her table. In the thick of the siege, one bullet passed through her bonnet and another through her bread tray. A long scar on her cheek was attributed to a Mexican saber encountered at Matamoros. These close calls did not deter her from service. She carried the wounded to the bombproof shelters and tended to their needs. She even asked for a musket of her own and joined the fray. Finally, after one solid week, the fighting subsided. The American army had held its ground, with only two dead and seventeen wounded.

The Eastern press was eager to print this story of the opening skirmish in the controversial frontier war. The fort was named after the fallen major, Jacob Brown, and Sarah Boujette gained another subtitle, the "Heroine of Fort Brown." The first full account of her patriotic service appeared, appropriately, in the Fourth of July edition of a Philadelphia newspaper. A story in a New York City newspaper followed soon after. The Great Western was the toast of the army and became a bona fide national legend.

After Matamoros, Taylor crossed the Rio Grande into Mexico and during the hot summer months marched across the Northeast Mexico desert. Sarah followed in her mule-rigged wagon, providing mess for twelve young officers. In late September the Mexicans and Americans clashed in Monterrey, with heavy casualties on both sides, but eventually the Americans were left to occupy the city. Sarah moved into one of the buildings, hired some young Mexican girls, and established an all-purpose lounge, restaurant, and procurement agency she called "The American House."

The American House was short-lived in Monterrey, as Taylor's army was soon heading southwest for the town of Saltillo. This was a larger city, taken without struggle. In Saltillo Sarah reestablished The American House and did brisk business. She was known for fixing grub at any hour of the night if a soldier came in hungry. The American House was, according to one soldier, "the headquarters for everybody." It was also, of course, a first-class bordello.

Sarah saw action in the next major battle, which took place a short distance away from Saltillo, in Buena Vista. It was a two-day, drawn-out, tooth-and-nail skirmish, with the apparent advantage shifting from Taylor's forces to General Santa Ana's and back. Once again, Sarah stepped into the battle to nurse the wounded, dressing their wounds, and even carrying them off the battlefield. Once again, she brought hot coffee to the troops and prepared food to sustain them.

At one point during this two-day siege, Sarah was back at her Saltillo restaurant when an underachieving Indiana private dashed in breathless with the news that Taylor was whipped, the army bust to pieces, and the Mexicans on the march. Sarah hauled off and decked him. Standing above the sprawled-out body, she delivered a few choice words and then declared, "There ain't Mexicans enough in Mexico to whip old Taylor. You just spread that rumor and I'll beat you to death."

A different piece of news Sarah received from behind the line inspired a wholly different response. She was told that Captain Lincoln had been shot and killed. Amid the smoke and din of battle, she searched for his body. Afterward, the matter of selling his gallant white horse arose. When someone bid $75 for it, Sarah counted that an indignity and bid $200, with the plan of returning the horse to Lincoln's family at the earliest opportunity. Sarah's code of honor was not for everyone, but it certainly had its rigorous moments.

After Taylor's victory in Buena Vista, the decisive battle in the northern Mexican campaign, Sarah returned to her business pursuits. Revelries at the unofficial headquarters must have gotten out of hand, because a new decree came down: "There shall not be a drop of liquor of any kind sold or kept at the establishment."

Mr. Boujette had faded from the picture by this time, but Sarah was evidently not fazed by this until the following year, when the Treaty of Guadalupe Hidalgo ended the war. The troops were headed on to points west to defend travelers seeking gold and profit in California from Mexicans and outlaws along the way. The leaders decided that women not married to military men could not travel with the company. As the troops assembled to depart, Sarah approached the commanding officer for permission to follow in the camp, and it was then that she learned of this regulation.

Without batting an eye she rode up to the line and addressed them thus: "Who wants a wife with $15,000 and the biggest leg in Mexico! Come, my beauties, don't all speak at once—who is the lucky man?"

One brave private came forward and said, "I have no objections to making you my wife, if there is a clergyman here who would tie the knot."

MY TASK IN LIFE IS TO BE A HAPPY WOMAN.
—Sally Conners, Montana horsewoman

To which The Great Western replied, "Bring your blanket to my tent tonight and I will learn you to tie a knot that will satisfy you, I reckon!"

Thus, for two short months, she became Sarah Davis, a legitimate army laundress once again. Then, on a march north through Chihuahua, they came across a well-armed party from Santa Fe, their ultimate destination. On the banks of the river Yaqui, along which grew peach trees loaded with ripe, golden fruit, Sarah's eyes lit upon a man fully her equal in size. In the words of one observer, The Great Western "saw this Hercules while he was bathing and conceived a violent passion for his gigantic proportions. She sought an interview and with blushes 'told her love.' "

Then, when the demigod indicated his willingness, she "straightaway kicked Davis out of her affections and tent, and established her elephantine lover in full possession without further ceremony."

In the throes of passion, Sarah dropped out of history for eight months. She resurfaced in the hamlet of Franklin (the future El Paso), an important crossroads for travelers taking a southern route to California. She had resumed her original married name of Boujette, as well as her bordello business. This made her, according to one historian, the first Anglo property owner in the West Texas town. According to another she was its first "prostitute of record."

Sarah seemed to have an aura that protected her from the hazards of frontier life. Indians and outlaws alike were awed into a respectful distance by her epic proportions and sexuality, not to mention her apparent willingness to use the guns she carried. She made do with the erratic availability of provisions and consistently gave an impression of kindness to Anglo travelers who stayed with her. Even her customers commonly approached her in a "polite, if not humble, manner."

El Paso grew quickly, too quickly for Sarah's taste. She moved, this time away from the army, which had descended in great numbers and brought with it a wave of civilization. On she went, possibly by herself, possibly with a man named Juan Duran, to the town of Socorro in central New Mexico. By the 1850 census Sarah was living with Duran and five girls with the last name of Skinner—possibly orphans of the frontier, possibly employees. The youngest Skinner, Nancy, was listed as only two years old; she remained with Sarah as a cherished adoptive daughter.

Less than two years later, Sarah was on the move with another man, Albert Bowman, a soldier at least ten years younger than she, whom she soon married. Together they arrived at Yuma,

Arizona. Like El Paso, Yuma was a southern gateway to California, situated where the Gila and Colorado Rivers meet. Sarah Bowman would spend nearly fifteen years associated with the fort at this crossroads.

At first Sarah worked as hospital matron and mess cook for army brass at the fort. The journal of a commanding officer, Major Samuel Peter Heintzelman, gives testimony to the forty-year-old woman's capacity to intrigue, arouse, and infuriate members of the opposite sex. After months of scribbling observations of Sarah in his journal, including the disparaging remarks of others about her mess, Heintzelman agreed to subscribe and tentatively found the meals satisfactory, especially when spiced with the woman's comments on his rivals. But when he tried to sell his stock animals to her, their friendship, as it was, fairly foundered. Evidently Sarah could drive a hard bargain.

Then she played upon this poor, bewildered man's affections. Telling the major that some strangers in San Diego were laying claim to her daughter Nancy, she enlisted his help in establishing a hotel across the river in Mexico, outside of U.S. jurisdiction, where Nancy might be seized. Evidently, Sarah was more interested in putting some distance between herself and her customers, for she immediately slacked off on the mess schedule. "The Western is making a convenience of us," the Major wrote. "She gives us what she pleases to eat and spends the whole day across the river." He got over it. He had little choice; hers was the only such service in town.

Sarah and Albert moved around Arizona a bit, from Tucson to Sonoita Creek, still on the military gravy train. In each new outpost she set up a hotel. Then gold was struck near Yuma, and the two returned to the fort. In 1864 Albert ran off with a much younger woman, leaving the legend to her admirers. By this time Sarah had adopted several Mexican and Indian children into her household. She spoke fluent Spanish with them, teaching them to cook and do laundry.

Sarah often said that there was just one thin sheet of sandpaper between Yuma and hell. She spoke either of local morality or the sandy ground she scratched to raise vegetable crops for the hotel. Legend has it that she died of a tarantula bite—a fitting image of the end of a rough frontier life. Everyone in Yuma turned out for the funeral. Memories of her bravery in battle were second only to professions of the kindness received at her hand. She was buried in Yuma. In 1980 her body was removed, along with the buried remains of soldiers, to be interred in the presidio in San Francisco.

Mary Ann "Molly" Dyer Goodnight

(1839–1926)

Mother to the Buffalo

Molly Goodnight heard the boom of the rifles that meant buffalo hunters were on the Llano Estacado, the "staked plains" of the Texas panhandle. She was surprised there were still buffalo to be had. Several years earlier, Molly had seen the herds on her trip west to Colorado with her cattleman husband, Charles Goodnight. But she had also heard of sport hunters killing as many as one-thousand animals in a month. And she had smelled the rotting carcasses on the wind. Molly was one of the first women to settle in this region of the plains and was a rare female witness to the savage buffalo hunts that left thousands of carcasses rotting on the plains.

By 1878 fewer than one hundred of the giant beasts survived in Texas, and the hunt was essentially over. One day that same year, Molly Goodnight, from the "JA" home ranch in the Palo Duro Canyon, heard the plaintive cries of

what she thought were wounded animals and set out with her gun to find them. Had they been badly injured, she would have to put them out of their pain. But the animals, two baby bison, were not wounded at all. Not far from them lay two skinned carcasses, black with flies. The calves bellowed; they had lost their mothers.

Molly had never seen buffalo calves at such a close range because their mothers usually protected them so fiercely. Her long cotton skirts rustled the grasses as she approached the beasts. The calves were skittish—after all, they were wild—but Molly turned away with her mind made up. The carcasses would attract lions and bobcats, putting the calves in further danger. She rode out on the range to find her husband and asked him to rope the calves and bring them back to the home ranch.

At first Charles opposed her. The elimination of the buffalo was, in part, what had made his enormous cattle business possible. But Molly did not give up. Though she was never domineering, she often got her way. And she knew her husband well. There was nothing the two liked better to do than to ride out together in the canyon to observe the wildlife. Surely he could not be indifferent to the bison. "Think of it as an exciting experiment," she told him. Charles agreed.

In decades to come, the buffalo would become the signature of the Goodnight ranch. These orphaned calves were the beginning of the first domestic buffalo herd, an important first in wildlife conservation. Equally important, they played a part in preserving the culture of the Plains Indians.

Mary Ann "Molly" Dyer was born to a prominent Tennessee family in 1839. She was followed by five brothers. When she was fourteen, her parents moved the family to Fort Belknap in Parker County, Texas. Forty miles to the west was a temporary reservation the federal government had set up for the Indians, mostly Comanches, who were "suffering with extreme hunger bordering on starvation" from the degradation of their hunting grounds. In 1859 an ex-Indian-agent stirred up raids and racial hatred on both sides, which led to much fighting. One of Molly's brothers died in these battles.

When her parents died, Molly cared for her remaining brothers and eventually became a schoolteacher to provide for the youngest of them. On the way to a new post in Weatherford, Molly first met Charles. She was traveling with an entourage of soldiers, for it was 1864, and the possibility of a Comanche raid was real.

Suddenly, on horseback before her was Charles Goodnight, already well known as a hardworking cattleman and a fearless Indian fighter. In fact he had been with the group of Texas Rangers who had "rescued" Cynthia Ann Parker from Comanches four years before. Ironically, years later he would develop a friendship with Quanah, Cynthia's son, while on the Palo Duro ranch. After the day he and Molly met on the trail, Charles made a habit of visiting the Weatherford schoolteacher.

Charles Goodnight was not the only man attracted by Molly's grace, intelligence, and good cheer. He courted Molly for five years before he was in the position to make a marriage proposal that the sought-after Molly might accept. He lacked formal education, but he made up for it in drive and ability.

He had spent those years away from cattle-rich Texas, driving herds into New Mexico, Colorado, and Wyoming, where the animals were more valued. After their wedding in Kentucky among

Dyer relatives, Molly joined him on his new ranch in Pueblo, Colorado. Molly's three youngest brothers, now grown into young men, were invited to come along to try out the ranching life.

As Molly and her modest entourage entered the town of Pueblo, the first thing they saw were the bodies of two outlaws dangling from a telegraph pole. A posse had caught and hanged them without trial. For Molly, whose father had been attorney general of Tennessee, vigilante "justice" was anathema. In Texas she had lived as an independent, single woman despite the threat of Indian raids. Living with outlaws and lynch mobs seemed worse. She asked to return to Texas immediately.

Her husband had to scramble to make their new home seem more civilized than it was. He introduced Molly to another woman in whom she found what she called "human qualities"— evidently more than could be said for some of the local men. As Charles Goodnight's business enterprises expanded into banking, real estate, and mining, Molly founded the town's first Southern Methodist Church so that Sunday mornings might be properly spent in the worship of God.

Hard times visited the West with the financial collapse of 1873, coming on top of an already difficult year of drought. Molly went to stay with relatives in California while Charles returned to Texas to plan his next move.

Charles visited Molly in 1876, full of plans. A Mexican guide had led him to a gorgeous natural region in the Texas Panhandle. He had immediately recognized the wide Palo Duro Canyon as an ideal place to run a cattle ranch. He staked his claim and found a partner in the Irish financier John George Adair. All this backer asked was that the ranch be named after him.

Charles and his men started the "JA Ranch" while Molly was still in California. She sent Charles a message, telling him if he didn't join her out in "civilization," she would come join him at the Palo Duro ranch. When he did not respond right away, Molly wrote again, "I will be in Denver a week after you get this letter. Meet me there." Ready or not, Charles had no choice.

A travel party made up of Molly, Charles, John Adair, his wife Cornelia, and four others headed out of Denver in 1877. Cornelia, a hardy horsewoman, rode a large white horse the whole way. Molly chose instead to drive a wagon. At one point she mistook a patch of beargrass for a band of Indians on the horizon. Obviously, Molly still harbored strong fears of her nomadic neighbors.

The canyon where they were headed was once a prime Comanche hunting ground. Besides hunting buffalo there, the Comanches had used the canyon walls to contain a herd of mustangs. In 1874 federal troops had slaughtered the mustangs and defeated the Comanches, ending forever their dominance there. It is appropriate that Molly's rescue of the buffalo occurred in a place so sacred to the Indians.

The party arrived safely at Palo Duro, and the Adairs left after two weeks. Though they had made the ranch possible, they put a strain on Molly's natural hospitality. One day a cowboy sat down at the dinner table, as their cowboys always had in Colorado. John Adair complained that he and "Lady Adair" could not sit at the table with a servant. As the cowboy got up to leave, Molly fired back that anyone who was good enough to work on their ranch was good enough to sit at her table. The cowboy returned to his seat, and John Adair took Cornelia to another table.

Molly cheerfully made do while Charles and his men built a cabin and corrals. He had brought some 1,800 cattle to the canyon on his first trip. Several outpost men guarded the canyon's opening to ensure that the cattle did not leave and that the buffalo they had driven out did not reenter the canyon.

Molly wholly embraced her new home. Compared to the sparse vegetation of the surrounding plains, the canyon was thick with shrubs and wildflowers. It was named for the palo duro, or cedar tree, which, along with the chinaberry and cottonwood trees, provided blessed shade in the summertime. With her house backed up to a canyon wall, she was protected from the relentless winds that discouraged so many plainswomen. Of course, there were rattlesnakes and other creatures to fear. One morning, Molly was brushed aside by a small stampede of buffalo. But there were innumerable delights, as well: the sociable, if pesky, prairie dogs, the brilliant-red cardinal flower, fresh wild berries, the enormous blue sky overhead, and the sun, every morning, as it warmed the ruddy canyon walls.

Molly's early training caring for her brothers served her well on the ranch. Though she never had children, she was maternal by habit and at ease with the ranch hands. The cowboys loved her—she was smart, attractive, thoughtful, and she could cook! She often rode out to the men on the distant lines to deliver berry cobblers or cakes. When the men came to stay at the home camp, Molly repaired britches and darned socks as she listened to their complaints or soothed their aches with home remedies. The cowboys began to call her "Aunt Molly" to express their affection and gratitude for all her small acts of caring.

Molly's popularity earned her the title of "Mother of the Panhandle: Darling of the Plains." Her influence, as well as her husband's strict rules, made for a well-behaved crew, not disposed to drinking or cardplaying. She was never too busy to sit down with one of the boys for a lesson in reading and writing.

Two artifacts attest to the men's affection for her. The JA Ranch cowboys saved their money to present her with a silver tea service, symbolic both of the "civilization" she brought to Palo Duro and of her enduring hospitality. Another gift she received was a tall clock from her husband, inscribed in her honor with these words: "For many months in 1877–78, she saw few men and no women, her nearest neighbor being seventy-five miles distant, and the nearest settlement two hundred miles. She met isolation and hardships with a cheerful heart and danger with undaunted courage. With unfailing optimism, she took life's varied gifts and made her home a house of joy."

One day, a cowboy presented her with something just as thoughtful: a sack containing three live chickens. Assuming that the chickens were for eating, she made a reference to the next day's dinner. The cowboy quickly corrected her. The chickens were for her to keep as pets. She later described the odd satisfaction of their companionship, "No one can ever know what a pleasure those chickens were to me, and how much company they were. They would come when I called them and they would follow me wherever I went, and I could talk to them."

Molly is said to have been a first-rate natural historian, conversant with the wildlife native to the canyon. Her days of solitude were spent not only chatting with the highbred chickens at home, but also on the trails observing prairie chickens and curlews and taking mental note of the succession of plants and grasses. She studied plants used in teas, tonics, salves, and compresses, learning when they flowered and scattered their seed and which seeds would grow where, and why.

All this helped her survive the fearful loneliness she experienced. She once said, "If there had been no outside dangers, the loneliness would not have been so bad." She was referring mainly to the threat of Indian raids, which haunted her imagination in the early years. Nature supplied other dangers. Her attentiveness to her surroundings was a matter of survival as well as enrichment.

Charles shared Molly's love of the natural world, taking interest in everything from turtles to cactus and frost-resistant peaches. Riding together on the open range, they must have had quite a lot to talk about. For such long excursions the

traditional sidesaddle proved uncomfortable, so Charles fashioned a sidesaddle with an extra horn on which Molly might brace her knee.

Within a year of the founding of JA Ranch, Quanah Parker and his band began to raid the Goodnight cattle herd. Molly was frantic to learn that Charles had gone out to speak with the leader. She barricaded the doors to her cabin with furniture. But both were reasonable men, not the kind of men who had incited so much hatred in the past. Charles had never hunted buffalo for sport; he had only driven them out of the canyon.

In a peace talk Charles confronted Quanah with genuine compassion as well as political savvy. He told him that the Comanches' quarrel was with the state of Texas, not with him. No, he was from Colorado. It was a "little white lie," but it made peace possible. If Quanah's people could not find buffalo, they were welcome to Goodnight beef, as many as two a day, to satisfy their hunger.

Molly eventually got used to the idea of Indians near the canyon. It was hard for her not to think of them occasionally as she was feeding the buffalo calves in their pens. Years later, after the buffalo herd had grown to a considerable number and the Comanches had settled in Indian Territory, Charles Goodnight invited Quanah and friends to return to the canyon for an old-fashioned buffalo hunt. It was an opportunity that helped the Comanches preserve the knowledge of their traditions.

At its height of productivity in 1885, the main ranch in Palo Duro Canyon had nearly fifty houses, hundreds of miles of roads, twenty or thirty large water tanks, just as many corrals, and two-thousand bulls. It had its own farm for producing hay, a dairy, and a poultry house stocked with a variety of breeds, a tin house, and a blacksmith's shop. The main house was a two-story wooden structure, with water fed through iron pipes. The mess house was a "large and very substantial" structure where young men did the cooking.

Improved technology as much as anything had brought scores more farmers and ranchers to the region, and all the trade that followed. With the invention of barbed wire, would-be ranchers did not need to find a natural barrier, such as the canyon, to contain their herds. And water could be pumped from underground with windmills, enabling subsistence farmers as well as ranchers to settle in the Panhandle.

But the depression of the mid-1880s squeezed large and small alike, and it forced Molly and Charles to leave the canyon ranch to the Adairs and move to a smaller ranch near the town of Goodnight on the prairie. Named after Charles, by now a famous rancher, the town had started as a station on the Fort Worth and Denver railroad line.

Now approaching her fiftieth birthday, Molly was ready to return to town. She threw herself into the life of Goodnight. Much to her husband's chagrin, her house was opened wide to people of all ages from beggars to celebrities, providing a center of cultural and social life. She initiated projects to encourage conservation of native plants and to educate Texans about the buffalo. As in Colorado, she built a church, but Charles never joined.

In 1898 Molly's dream of founding a college was realized. At Goodnight College, situated just over the hill from the Goodnights' new ranch, the region's youth came to take junior-college courses. They could pay for their tuition with beef or by working in the garden and dairy that provided the school's food. Mary Ann Dyer Goodnight became "Aunt Molly" to an entirely new group of young men and women, nurturing the students as she had the cowboys. In 1910, however, a larger normal college was opened several miles away, and Goodnight College enrollment quickly declined.

The reduction in their landholdings forced the Goodnights to cut back on cattle, but they always kept the buffalo, increasing the herd to 250 head. The Goodnight buffalo herd gained international attention when Charles began breeding "cattalo," a hardy cross between the plains and pasture animals.

By the end of the century, buffalo had become more valuable alive than dead; Goodnight buffaloes were sent to the New York Zoo, to Yellowstone National Park, and even to Europe. Buffalo hides, mounted heads, and meat became novelty items that only the wealthy could afford. Of course, the herd that Molly had started was also a major attraction for passersby and visitors to their large new home.

At the end of Molly's life, her house was a combined museum and bed-and-breakfast. Indian artifacts—found, given as gifts, or purchased on trips to reservations—were displayed side by side with the objects from the ranching heydays. She gave many tours herself, a fitting finale to an eventful life. She had witnessed and participated in much of the drama of early Texas history; it was written in her days and years and in her memory, and she was happy to share it with others. Molly Ann Dyer Goodnight died in 1926.

ANY WOMAN WHO THIRSTS TO WEAR TROUSERS AND RIDE
BRONCOS IS A VICTIM OF A CURIOUS MENTAL DISORDER.

—*The New York Times*, May 27, 1876

Mary Louise Cecilia "Texas" Guinan

(1884–1933)

The Notorious Hostess

"Hello, suckers!" The big, brassy, peroxide-blond woman, draped with gaudy jewelry and caked with makeup, huskily greeted the crowd through the smoky haze that had already wrapped the tables into an exotic intimacy. Prohibition was in effect in New York, but "Tex," innovator of the nightclub scene, was out to entertain her customers as they slid into inebriation. Entertainment was not her sole purpose; she was also out to rake in their cash, as her trademark greeting suggested. Her well-oiled racket raised about $4,000 a week from the city slickers who seemed eager to pay $1.50 for a glass of ginger ale—at the time, equivalent to a few hours' wages! So let 'em, thought Tex. Give 'em a good time, and nobody would ask questions—except, of course, possibly the police.

Tex had the Texan gift of thinking big: "Exaggerate the world," she would say. "Dress up your lives with imagination . . . don't lose that purple mantle of illusion. It's worth more than the price of admission. . . ."

So Tex would tell a few jokes and chat with the customers, rather like today's late-night talk-show hosts—and late night was about the time that her evenings began. She'd introduce her bevy of dancing girls, "Now how about a big hand for the little ladies?" She'd bring the biggest spenders onstage and ask for applause. She'd get to know people and give them whatever they wanted. And, sometimes, she'd tell stories about herself.

Later, she wrote about herself in her syndicated newspaper column:

Altogether I had the happiest gayest sort of childhood—between spanks—any young American could have. Roping steers and helping the boys round up the horses were chores which I learned at an early age. I wore pants like my brothers all day long, and except when caught and sent to school I was tearing around the ranch on a horse.

That active outdoor life is responsible for my unusual good health and endurance at present. A city bred girl would never survive the arduous life I have led, and still lead.

It was a glorious feeling to lope or gallop my pinto across miles of plains with the hot wind blowing my long yellow curls out in a straight line behind me. And it never occurred to me to be proud of my freedom at such a tender age. It simply seemed natural to ride. It was the life of the Texas plain.

One day, she claimed, she heard that Hank Miller's Wild West circus was coming to town. She decided to go and show the boys some tricks, and by the time she had finished putting her bronco, Pedro, through his paces, she'd been hired as a traveling performer. Between her shows, she said, she'd wander the grounds and study human nature, absorbing Barnum's business adage that "there's a sucker born every minute." The truth of this circus story is questionable because more scrupulous biographers have noted that Miller's circus didn't even exist when Tex was a girl.

Mary Louise Cecilia Guinan was born and raised in the great cattle-and-cotton crossroads town of Waco. She was 100 percent Irish; both her parents were Canadian-born children of immigrants. They had met in Colorado; the same love of adventure that had taken them there inspired a move to Texas. Michael Guinan was a half-successful merchant—ambitious and perhaps a touch too romantic for the trade. When his daughter was six, he lost his grocery to speculation. Bessie Guinan was a devout Catholic and a dedicated wife and mother, teaching "Mayme," as Tex was called growing up, the social graces. Bessie dressed her daughter in the voluminous female garments of late-1880s fashion, and Mayme, despite the emergence of her tomboy character, loved the fuss and bustle. The two were so devoted that the family took to calling the mother "Big Mayme," a sure sign of whose was the dominant character.

Although surrounded by cattle culture and people of the frontier, Mayme grew up in a town of twelve-thousand, not on her fantasized ranch. Her early escapades involved climbing trees with her younger brothers, not riding bareback on the plains. When she reached school age, her parents enrolled her in the local convent school, where she proved to be quite a handful. Outside school some of her favorite pranks included ordering bakery goods for fictitious customers and trying on shoes she had no intention of buying. Inside, the nuns were shocked by her frank and earthy talk. So notorious was she that some of the upper-crust parents of her class-mates forbade their daughters to associate with her. Mayme indulged her imagination with stories of heroic girls. Once, so she said, she kidnapped a neighbor's baby so that she could "save" it from harm the way one of her book heroines had saved an infant—by taking it across the river in a leaky boat. The wooden washtub she used did indeed leak, but the swollen Brazos River behind her house ran so fast that both "heroine" and baby had to be rescued themselves.

Even her most skeptical biographer has reason to believe that she may have been involved with a circus. There is no arguing that Mayme was a fine horsewoman, as her later performances in silent films showed her to be. Circus interlude or not, by the time Mayme reached fourteen, Big Mayme had planned another destiny for her daughter. Motherhood was every woman's calling, Big Mayme thought, and the first step to motherhood was finding a man. One summer, Bessie Guinan took her daughter west to Idaho Springs, Colorado, to stay several months at her sister's house; another summer, they went to Anaconda, Montana, to visit another set of relatives. Mayme enjoyed great success in these social training grounds. According to one Anaconda miner's tale, she "glorified in her swarm of beaux . . . [she] was always very much in demand and Mother was always there." In 1900, the year Mayme turned sixteen, the family moved permanently to Denver. There, according to the *Denver Post*, she "stormed the social fort and gained admission." She became known for wearing evening gowns to Sunday church services; at the same time she was gaining attention for her roles in local theater productions. But before Mayme's theatrical career could be properly launched, Big Mayme's influence won out: Her daughter married a Mr. John J. Moynahan and moved with him to Chicago.

Within two years the irrepressible Mayme had left "Moy" to pursue her dreams in New York City, counting on her talent and her big personality to forge an entertainment career. She didn't have much trouble finding success. One person whom she attracted was Hannah Boyer, an African American laundress who "borrowed" her wealthy customers' dresses to keep her friend looking snazzy. Onstage, "Miss Guinan," as she was known to reviewers, capitalized on the reputation of her home state. One evening while she was performing a vaudeville singing act as the

"Lone Star Novelty," she noticed the prominent Broadway producer John Slocum in the audience. As he rose to leave in the middle of a number, she stopped and shone her flashlight on him. "If you're going out, bring one back for me!" she declared. In fact, she never drank, but the audience loved the gag. Slocum stayed; he too was hooked, and he took over management of her career. It was he who shaped her as "Texas Guinan" and pampered her and coached her to think like a star.

A review from the *Los Angeles Times* of one of her Slocum show tours provides a striking character sketch of a young woman overfond of attention:

Miss Texas Guinan is in the budding prima donna stage. Her whimsical little egotisms are calling loudly for a strong stage manager to put an end to them. A pretty and vivacious girl, she loves the spotlight too much. She would make better use of her voice if she did not try for so many effects. And finally, she would appear to be more in the play if she would address herself more to the people of the stage and less to the front.

Tex, as she came to be known, was so insulted she insisted that Slocum demand an apology.

The critic, Julian Johnson, would not hear of apologizing. Months later, when Tex was again in Los Angeles, she recounted the story at a luncheon she was attending, this time without Slocum. "If that Julian Johnson ever meets up with me, he is in for some hard luck," she told her unknown lunch partner. The man sitting across from her laughed and invited her to dinner. After he had left, the host informed Tex that her partner had been none other than Julian Johnson. Tex laughed heartily. It was the beginning of a long, loving relationship, but the two never married.

Tex was just beginning to enjoy the financial rewards of stardom when she made an unwise business deal. Known for her battles with weight gain, she formed a partnership with a businessman to sell diet pills bearing her name. The man proved to be a fraud, and Tex lost much of what she had earned up to that point.

Before World War I the silent film was just gaining a foothold in the United States, and nowhere more than in Los Angeles, where Tex had a home with Johnson. After the war the industry exploded as the new form of entertainment became very popular. Tex embraced it as a perfect vehicle for her public persona and eventually formed her own, short-lived production company. Her films were, of course, westerns, but Tex was a unique leading lady. Not for her were the traditional "damsel in distress" roles, but neither did she play wicked women or femmes fatales. Rather, she became the divided heroine—the woman who could ride, shoot, and rescue, but whose heart was as weak as any other woman's. This departure from convention became her special draw.

In the 1919 film *Girl of the Rancho,* one of the few Texas Guinan films now available on video, Tex plays an "orphaned" (fatherless) woman named Texas Carroll, whose cherished little sister is named Waco. When she rebuffs the romantic advances of a Mexican bandit, the Mexican and his friends kidnap Waco after tying up Tex and her mother. Having freed herself, she mounts her white horse and takes off after them. Meanwhile, a group of white cowboys has intercepted the bandits. Arriving at the scene of the showdown, Tex climbs a bluff with her pistol and lariat. The lead bandit threatens to kill Waco if the white cowboys shoot, but Tex is able to rope her sister and lift her from his clutches. The white men prevail, and in the final scene, their handsome leader gravitates toward the buxom, jowly heroine.

In a 1920 film, *The White Squaw,* a woman named Texas Caswell dreams of the West from the cabin she shares with her brother Tom.

When the "revenooer," or lawman, shows up at their house accusing Tom of bootlegging, he takes offense and ties him to his horse backwards before sending him in the direction of the real bootleggers. But Tex worries for his safety and rides after him.

She unties him and returns to the cabin, where the bootleggers have gathered in anger at Tom for his betrayal. Tex disguises herself in the clothing of a man she has shot and runs to join her brother in the cabin. Eventually, the lawman shows up with his men and sets things in order. At the end Tex only looks dreamily at him; then the film cuts to a family tableau of the lawman, Tex, and a young boy, their son.

After appearing in many movies, Tex eventually tired of "kissing horses in horse operas" and returned to New York in 1922. Prohibition had launched the era of the speakeasies—dark, basement-level clubs where liquor was available and patrons needed passwords to enter. At age thirty-eight Tex was about to create a new form of entertainment, the nightclub. Just for fun she began to bring her showbiz friends to Gypsyland, a Hungarian restaurant where her friend Joe Fejer had been hired to play violin. Word spread, and others flocked to enjoy the party. The owner of

WHEN YOU ARE LOOKING FOR SOMETHING TO EAT, A RATTLESNAKE CAN DO JUST FINE.

**—Mary S. Hawkins,
Wyoming Territory, 1899**

the Café des Beaux Arts saw how well Fejer and Tex worked together and hired them to host the evening entertainment at his restaurant.

Tex did exactly what her mother had taught her to do: Play the gracious hostess, make people feel relaxed. She greeted her guests by name, if she knew them, and learned their names if she didn't. Tex was the emcee, with help from Fejer and a few dancers, but the real entertainment was provided by whoever decided to show up. Soon, an ex-taxicab-driver-turned-rumrunner named Larry Fay approached Tex about forming a partnership and running their own club. The El Fay was born at the corner of Forty-fifth Street and Sixth Avenue.

Everyone came around, including news reporters looking for leads, looking for action. Literary types like Ring Lardner would show up. Claire Luce and others got their start there as dancers. And, of course, there were the suckers. Everyone there was a sucker; anyone who would pay the cover charge of $6.00 or more had to be. But nobody seemed to mind. "Hello, suckers," Tex would say, and they'd all warm up to her. Then there was the "big butter-and-egg man." Tex came up with this phrase to describe a big spender who distributed $50 bills to her girls. Every night he showed up, she would call him

WHEN (MALE COMPETI-TORS IN A SHOOTING COMPETITION) SAW ME COMING ALONG THEY LAUGHED AT THE NOTION OF MY SHOOT-ING AGAINST THEM.... IT KIND OF GALLED ME TO SEE THOSE HULKING CHAPS SO TICKLED IN WHAT WAS NO DOUBT TO THEM MY IMPERTI-NENCE IN DARING TO SHOOT AGAINST THEM--AND I RECKON I WAS TICKLED TOO WHEN I WALKED AWAY WITH THE PRIZE.

—Annie Oakley

the "big butter-and-egg man." Soon others were vying for the honor.

Sometimes, of course, the cops came, sent folks home, and padlocked the doors. For several years it was a game of cat and mouse. One club would be shut down and another would open. Fay learned the loopholes of the law, keeping the liquor in a separate building and serving it only to regular customers. In response the New York Police Department gave its detectives enough cash to behave like big spenders, earn the club's trust, and then bust it. Then came the curfew laws: Places had to be closed at three o'clock, just when things were warming up at Tex's place. When the cops would show up, Tex would banter with them. The raids became just another part of the entertainment.

About this time Tex began writing an opinion column in the *New York Graphic,* a tabloid, and produced a Broadway show called Padlocks of 1927. In June of 1928 Tex's 300 Club was part of the biggest raid on nightclubs ever in New York. She was arrested and declared a public nuisance. During her trial she testified, probably truthfully, that she had never had a drop of alcohol and claimed she wouldn't know it if she saw it. Fay had indeed kept her out of the bootlegging side of the business. She described her job this way: "There was always something doing every minute. My duties were to see that everybody had a good time and that everything came off."

And in this case she got off. The jury was swayed by the fact that the accusing officers had attended the club for eight or twelve visits each, spending a total of $360 in taxpayer funds, though a couple of them professed not to like the scene. A huge celebration ensued the night Tex was acquitted. The celebration carried over to a film project, Queen of the Night Clubs. Her memoir, *My Life, and How!,* began syndication in the *New York Evening Standard.*

Texas's next adventure was a trip to Paris with her dancing girls. The other entertainers in Paris, probably worried about losing customers, agitated against her receiving a work permit. In effect her troupe was deported, but they returned home triumphant as the "Too Hot for Paris" Traveling Show and began to travel from club to club on a large bus. That tour was interrupted one evening when the legendary gangster Dutch Schultz showed up in Tex's dressing room and demanded she stop the performance. They'd had a run-in before her departure when she had fired a showgirl with whom Schultz was involved. The event was complicated by the fact that one of Schultz's men managed the club where they were supposed to perform. Tex quickly changed clubs, but this proved that it was getting to be a dangerous time for bootleggers and their associates. While Tex was abroad, Larry Fay, her former partner, had been murdered.

Toward the end Tex's life took an unexpected turn. She became obsessed with the noted evangelist Aimee Semple McPherson Hutton, and after a short debate with her on religion and women's role, Tex challenged her to another debate on a topic of Aimee's choice. The evangelist refused, but Tex persisted, offering to send the proceeds to a needy cause. The offer was typical of Tex's spiritual work; while she brought a kind of joie de vivre to the rich, she frequently performed benefits for the poor. Meanwhile, Aimee's religious revivals were solidly aimed at the middle class. When Aimee's refusal proved firm, Tex went to her church, "got religion," and told the press of her sincere desire to preach. "I want to invest my time and efforts in spreading sunshine, happiness, and blessing to others. . . . Happiness is the goal of all human achievement and that is what I intend to tell the world."

On a rigorous West Coast vaudeville tour, intended to familiarize herself with the "sawdust trail" of evangelism and raise money for charity, Tex was afflicted with severe abdominal pain and consulted a doctor in Portland. Finally, in Tacoma, she found a pastor who would allow her to preach the following Sunday. She planned her sermon carefully, typing out notes. She knew from her years as an entertainer how little money and material success meant to people. What mattered, she knew, were the little, childish things and giving others the best one had. Sunday arrived and, as she climbed into the pulpit, she saw a note that said her mother and God were listening. She delivered her sermon and broke into tears. According to the pastor her performance left no doubts about the sincerity of her message.

A week later Texas Guinan died of ulcerative colitis in Vancouver, British Columbia. It was November 5, 1933, exactly one month before the repeal of the Eighteenth Amendment marked the end of Prohibition and the end of the era in which Tex had become a legend.

Tex Guinan's flamboyant character has been portrayed in any number of films. She was played by Betty Hutton in *The Incendiary Blonde* (1945), a film based loosely on her fictional autobiography. The popular 1961 film *Splendor in the Grass* features a short appearance by Tex, as impersonated by Phyllis Diller. Most recently, Tex was played by Courtney Love in the Martin Scorsese film *Hello Sucker*.

Ann Bassett
(1878–1956)

Josie Bassett
(CA. 1874–1964)

Cattle-Rustling Queens

Ann Bassett had good reason to fear for her life. The owner of a small ranch in northwestern Colorado, she had watched for decades as trouble brewed between homesteaders and cattle barons over control of the open range. In 1900 two good friends had been murdered, one of them after finding a death threat pinned to his front gate. Now, only months later, Ann had received her own menacing, unsigned letter. It warned her to "leave that country for parts unknown within thirty days or you will be killed."

Ann and her friends figured they knew who was responsible for the letter, as well as for the mounting atrocities: the big cattle companies, which wanted to intimidate settlers into leaving the area so they could seize control of the grazing land and watering holes for their livestock. Ann was frightened, of course, but she was also stubborn. She refused to flee the state and instead avenged her friends' deaths by patrolling the range and killing any cattle from the big outfits that strayed into Brown's Park, where she and her neighbors lived and grazed their herds.

Eventually, the cattle corporations tried a different tactic. In 1911 they pressured the local sheriff into arresting Ann for rustling their cattle. The evidence was flimsy, and public sentiment was decidedly in favor of outspoken Ann, who made no secret of her belief that the "grasping cattle barons . . . were the biggest cattle thieves of all time."

In Craig, where the trial was to be held, townsfolk chipped in to rent the local opera house so more spectators could cram inside to listen to the proceedings. Ann was called to the stand as the final witness for the defense.

"Her hourglass figure beautifully dressed, her rich brown hair perfectly coiffed, [she] presented a picture of a maligned and abused lady being persecuted by evil men," according to biographer Grace McClure.

The trial ended in a hung jury. A second trial two years later ended in Ann's acquittal. Many westerners were ecstatic that she had won her feud with the powerful cattle barons. "Businesses Close, Bands Blare—Town of Craig Goes Wild with Joy!" screamed the headline in the Denver Post. Ann was "placed in an automobile and paraded through the main streets of the town receiving the congratulations and well wishes of her friends," according to the story that followed.

But many people, including some of Ann's friends, harbored no doubt that she had rustled a few cattle in her lifetime. No one protested—not even Ann—when a Denver reporter dubbed her the "Queen of the Cattle Rustlers." For the rest of her life she was proud to be known as "Queen Ann." The title paid homage to her showdown with the cattle barons, as well as to her regal bearing and imperious presence.

Ann wasn't the only Bassett who could lay claim to being a legend. Her mother, Elizabeth, founded the family ranch and ran it successfully at a time when ranching was considered a man's domain. Ann's sister Josie entered local lore as a gun-toting, self-sufficient pioneer who married and discarded five husbands, one of them under suspicious circumstances.

No more appropriate place could the hardy Bassett clan call home than Brown's Park, a 35-mile-long valley that straddles the border between northwestern Colorado and northeastern Utah. Isolated and sparsely populated, the area was a magnet for outlaws on the run in the late 1800s. Some, including Butch Cassidy, became fast friends of the Bassetts. As McClure said in her entertaining 1985 book *The Bassett Women:*

In this rustlers' hangout, surrounded by warring cattlemen, the Bassetts lived in a world of rustling and thievery, of lynching and other forms of murder. Their neighbors could comprise the standard cast of a Hollywood western: honest ranchers, rough and tough cowboys, worthless drifters, dastardly villains, sneaking rustlers, gentlemanly bank robbers, desperate outlaws, and ruthless cattle barons. Most Americans assume this world vanished long ago, yet people alive today remember Queen Ann striding along in her custom-made boots and Josie riding to town for supplies with her team and wagon.

Even though flanked by other fascinating frontier characters, the Bassett women commanded attention. They expected to be treated as men's equals—not because they wanted to change social mores, but because they believed that the freedom offered by the West was as much theirs as any man's. According to McClure, they had "audacity and strong will, high temper and obstinacy, good humor and open-handedness, unashamed sexuality— qualities that their contemporaries summed up as 'the Bassett charm.'"

Originally from Arkansas, the Bassett family migrated west in 1877 in search of a drier climate that would offer Herb, the sickly family patriarch, some relief from his asthma. They settled in Brown's Park, where Herb's brother Sam had been prospecting for more than twenty years. They soon discovered that the country, while handsome and invigorating, offered no instant riches.

Cattle fever was sweeping the West, and ambitious Elizabeth was soon infected. Cattle ranching, she believed, was her ticket to prosperity. Once she built a herd, she could fatten her livestock for free on thousands of square miles of public grasslands that until recently had supported buffalo.

However, there were risks to the cattle business. While lawmen turned a blind eye, rich and greedy cattle barons were snatching up what public grazing land they could, and many of them had no compunction about running off small ranchers and homesteaders who got in their way. Any settler who tried to fight back risked seeing his cabin and crops go up in flames. Worse yet, he might be lynched or shot in the back. But so far the cattle barons had shown little interest in the remote meadows of Brown's Park. So while Herb, a "little old maid of a man," served first as the local postmaster and then as justice of the peace, Elizabeth began building her herd.

The Bassetts also continued to build their family. Their first two children, Josie and Samuel, had been born in Arkansas. In 1878 Ann became the first known white child born in Brown's Park. A second Bassett son, Elbert, was born a year later. Elizabeth didn't have enough breast milk to nourish infant Ann, so she employed a Ute Indian mother as a wet nurse. Six months later, a family friend presented Ann with a milk cow.

"I got into the cow business at a decidedly early age," she later joked.

Ann did start cowboying early in life. At the age of six, she was herding cattle on horseback.

"I had the privilege of living in a bronco West," she later said. "My ambitions were centered upon an ability to flank a calf or stick a wild cow's head through a loop, as neatly as any of them."

When young Ann rode the range, fences were as rare as ships in the mountains. Cattle wandered far and wide, and there weren't enough cowboys to keep track of them. Ranchers expected to lose some animals to bad weather and predators, but they could not abide rustlers, who were experts at altering brands and rounding up unbranded mavericks.

In McClure's opinion a certain amount of

DON'T SCREW WITH ME, FELLAS. THIS AIN'T MY FIRST TIME AT THE RODEO.

—Lulu Parr

rustling was to be expected, perhaps even excused, given the "conditions under which [settlers] were struggling to survive."

"These illegal brandings . . . are as understandable as a slum kid's snitching an apple from a grocer's pile of fruit," she wrote.

Still, when rumors began to circulate that Elizabeth was building her herd by branding strays and buying cut-rate cattle from professional rustlers, one stockman disdainfully declared her the head of the "Bassett gang."

One of Elizabeth's ranch hands was Butch Cassidy, a good-natured young man who loved to read books from Herb's extensive library. Sometimes Cassidy went dancing with fifteen-year-old Josie on his arm. She once referred to him as her "Brown's Park beau," though in later years she coyly refused to confirm or deny any relationship. Ann adored Cassidy, too. As an eleven-year-old, she tailed him like a puppy as he did his chores.

A neighbor once saw the Bassett sisters get into a "knock-down, drag-out" fight as they argued over Cassidy's affections. When Ann was in her late teens, she apparently was a close companion of Cassidy, staying with him for a time at a hideout across the Utah border. Their relationship eventually cooled as the famous outlaw shifted his attention to other parts of the country and then fled to South America.

Back on the Bassett ranch, Elizabeth was developing considerable skill as a rancher. While blizzards in the winters of 1885 and 1887 destroyed bigger operations, her herd emerged as strong as ever. Her luck finally played out in 1892, when she apparently suffered a miscarriage and died at the age of thirty-seven. The Bassetts had lost their anchor—and their main source of income. Ann and Josie, still teenagers, knew they had to grow up quickly to survive on the unforgiving frontier.

Josie found the years after her mother's death especially trying. In 1894 she married Jim McKnight, one of three hands who had helped Elizabeth run the Bassett ranch. When McKnight, a longtime bachelor, began visiting a nearby saloon to escape the constraints of matrimony, Josie fumed. When McKnight proposed leaving their ranch, moving to Vernal, and opening a saloon of their own, Josie filed for divorce. She was not about to let a man come between her and her love of ranch life.

In April 1900 the conflict came to a head when a sheriff's deputy tried to serve McKnight with divorce papers. As strong willed and hot tempered as his wife, he refused to accept them and walked away. The deputy ordered McKnight to halt, then shot and badly wounded him when he refused.

Josie's second marriage lasted four years, and her third lasted just six months. Josie tried to cure her fourth husband, Emerson Wells, of a drinking problem by feeding him a medicine known as the Keeley Cure. Wells died suddenly after a New Year Eve's binge. Because of her checkered reputation, Josie was accused by gossipmongers of poisoning Wells, but they had no proof and never brought charges.

Now thirty-nine years old, Josie decided to homestead just over the Colorado-Utah border, at Cub Creek near Vernal. She made another bad choice in mates—a rude, crude man named Morris. After her new husband abused her horse, Josie chased him off with a frying pan.

Josie was a hard worker but always found it difficult to make ends meet. In the 1920s Prohibition offered her an enticing opportunity. She was not a drinker herself, but she had no qualms about making her living selling moonshine. She set up a still in the gulch below her cabin and brewed corn whisky and apricot brandy for the next several years, guaranteeing herself a steady source of income. Finally, her family prevailed on her to stop before she ended up in jail.

Though she had little money, Josie was always willing to help neighbors who had less than she did. She regularly loaded poached venison or rustled beef into her wagon and delivered it to hungry families.

"It is almost surprising that it was not until January 1936 that she was indicted for stealing cattle belonging to the ranchers who grazed their cattle" near her homestead, according to McClure. Josie was tried twice for rustling. Despite strong evidence, both juries acquitted the compassionate grandmother.

Even in her seventies, Josie pushed the boundaries of the law. She once got fed up with a neighbor's mule that had pestered her horses and killed her granddaughter's colt. So she lured the mule into the hills, shot it, and sent it tumbling to the bottom of a gully.

Life magazine learned of Josie's exploits and dispatched reporters to investigate in 1948. The resulting story depicted Josie as a salty, rifle-toting frontierswoman. It also called her the "Queen of the Cattle Rustlers," much to Ann's chagrin. The article inspired a 1967 movie, *The Ballad of Josie,* starring Doris Day.

Ann got her own moment in the media spotlight when she detailed her colorful life in articles in *Colorado Magazine* in 1952 and 1953.

With a penchant for elaboration, she didn't make it easy for readers to sort fact from fiction. In one story she claimed she roped a grizzly cub when she was just thirteen. The enraged grizzly sow chased Ann up a tree, she said, and then mauled her horse. Cowboys rode to the rescue and shot the mother bear, then gave Ann "the damnedest shaking" and licking a kid could ever get, she reported.

Ann spent part of her childhood at boarding schools in Salt Lake City and Boston, where she learned to appreciate culture. The tough tomboy who could bust a bronc could also quote Shakespeare.

"In the end she became a genuine curiosity," according to Colorado historians John H. Monnett and Michael McCarthy, "a frontier hybrid of both toughness and beauty, part poet, but part hellion too, who smelled at once of damp leather and eastern perfume, and who at all times remained an enigma to those around her."

When Ann was twenty-six, she shocked friends and foes alike by propositioning a cowboy named Hi Bernard, who was twenty years her senior. It wasn't so much the age difference that set tongues wagging; it was the fact that Bernard worked for the Bassetts' archrival, Ora Haley, a cattle baron who owned the immense Two-Bar

Ranch. Many folks, including Ann, believed that Haley had ordered the murders of two of the Bassetts' friends and neighbors. Still, Ann knew Bernard was one of the best cowmen in the country, and she needed his help to expand her own cattle business. Not surprisingly, Haley's wedding gift to Bernard was the frontier equivalent of a pink slip.

Young Ann soon became bored with her new husband. She started spending time in the company of a handsome cowboy, and Bernard moved to Denver. Ann later divorced him and married Frank Willis, an easygoing man who could tolerate her hot temper and freewheeling ways. When Ann knocked him out with a frying pan for coming home drunk one night, he simply shrugged off the incident.

Ann spent her days running the family ranch, mingling with outlaws, and repelling the cattle barons who tried to take over her land. She continued to live a hard and fast-paced life until 1953, when she suffered a severe heart attack. She died three years later, on May 8, 1956, at the age of seventy-eight.

Shortly before her death, she told a reporter, "I've done everything they said I did and a helluva lot more."

Josie continued to live alone at her homestead on Cub Creek, where there was no running water, electricity, or telephone. She spent fifty years in her cabin there and left at the age of eighty-nine, after suffering a broken hip when her horse knocked her down. Realizing she'd never be able to return home, she died in May 1964 at a Salt Lake City hospital.

Josie was buried near Ann and Elizabeth on the family homestead at Brown's Park. She was the last Bassett to be interred there. The family plot is not open to the public, but tourists can visit Josie's homestead and cabin at Dinosaur National Monument.

Josie and Ann both lived long enough to see the end of the frontier, but they stubbornly refused to change with the times. They never abandoned the spirit and the values they acquired on their homesteads. As McClure put it:

> Both women [carried] a combination of pioneer values and an utter disregard for any conventions that ran counter to their own standards of right and wrong. They were sometimes condemned by their more conservative contemporaries—understandably, for what they did was not always admirable. They lived their lives as they wished, doing what they wanted to do or what they felt they were compelled to do, with never a serious qualm when they overstepped the bounds of a "proper society."

Fannie Sperry Steele
(1887–1983)

Champion Bronc Rider

On September 1, 1912, the most ambitious rodeo of its time got off to a sour start. A steady drizzle soaked the corrals and exhibition grounds at Victoria Park in Calgary, Alberta, where the first Calgary Stampede was about to get underway. Cowboys in rain slickers hustled to and fro on the backs of dripping mounts. Supply wagons and milling livestock churned through the mud.

As twenty-five-year-old Fannie Sperry along with her mother Rachel gamely inspected the displays—including exact replicas of Old Fort Whoop-Up and the original Hudson's Bay Company trading post—a man burst out of one of the horse barns, shouting for a doctor. But it was too late. Cowboy Joe Lamar had just been thrown and trampled to death by a bronc with the deceptively innocuous name of Red Wing. Though she didn't know it, Fannie would soon have her own confrontation with the murderous beast.

Fannie Sperry had not come to Calgary to sit demurely on the sidelines and applaud the action. She had been invited to compete for the title of "Lady Bucking Horse Champion of the World." And she had every intention of winning.

The final day of the Stampede dawned clear and sunny. More than sixty thousand people crowded into the stands and watched as the Duke of Connaught—Governal General of Canada and uncle of the King of England—rode into the arena in an open coach pulled by two white horses. Wearing a uniform smothered in medals and a naval officer's hat crowned with a plume, he climbed into the royal box with his wife and daughter and settled down to watch the performance.

The male bronc riders went first, followed by exhibitions of stagecoach driving and rope tricks. Then came the finals of the women's bronc-riding competition. Each participant drew a slip of paper from a hat to determine which animal she would ride. Fannie drew the killer horse, Red Wing.

A more timid soul would have cringed at the prospect of climbing onto the back of one of the most dangerous horses in the bucking string, but Fannie was delighted. If she could stick to Red Wing, surely she would deserve the championship!

Fannie waited nervously as her competitors burst from the chutes atop a series of seething mounts. Finally it was her turn. The best, one of the judges announced, had been saved for last. Fannie Sperry of Mitchell, Montana, would attempt to ride the deadly bronc. Writer Dee Marvine described what happened next:

The glistening sorrel stood taut, and a shudder rippled across his flanks as Fannie eased into the saddle. Positioning the toes of

her boots in the stirrups, she adjusted her grip on the buck rein. The familiar feel of her own saddle provided small comfort, as she poised her body against the cantle, her legs gripping the horse's girth. She signaled, and the gate opened.

The ride that followed is recorded in rodeo annals as one of the best ever made by a woman—or a man. Fannie rode the murderous horse, never losing control, never sacrificing balance and style. When the hazer pulled her free in front of the royal box, a thundering ovation measured her triumph. She saluted the audience with a bow and a wide sweep of her hat.

The judges' decision was quick in coming. The first Lady Bucking Horse Champion of the World was none other than Fannie Sperry! Along with the title went a check for one thousand dollars, a gold buckle, a saddle hand-tooled with roses—and a reputation that would change her life.

Fannie Sperry was born March 27, 1887, in the shadow of the Bear Tooth, a mountain north of Helena, Montana Territory, that has since become known as the Sleeping Giant. Along with two brothers and two sisters, she grew up on the family ranch and was infected early on by her mother's love of horses. Even as a toddler, she later said, it was obvious which way her "twig was bent." Her mother often liked to tell the story of the day little Fannie waited by a spring, hoping one of the wild horses that roamed the hills behind the homestead would come to drink. When a maverick pinto approached, the toddler wielded a long scarf for a lasso and vowed to "tetch me a white-face horthie!" By the age of six, Fannie had a pony of her own.

Rachel Sperry had a no-nonsense way of teaching her children to ride. She simply plopped them onto the back of a gentle horse and told them not to fall off. If they disregarded the command, she gave them a smart smack on the behind and lifted them back into the saddle. By the time the Sperry children were teenagers, they were all expert riders capable of breaking and shoeing their own horses.

Fannie first rode for a paying audience in the summer of 1903, when she was only sixteen. She thrilled residents of Mitchell, a tiny settlement not far from the Sperry ranch, by sticking like a cocklebur to the back of a writhing, white stallion. Her black braids and free right hand swung like horsewhips as the animal tried to buck her off. Onlookers were so impressed that they passed a hat and gave her all the money that was collected.

A year later, Fannie began her professional riding career—not as a bronc rider, but as a relay racer. Patterned after the Pony Express race that Buffalo Bill Cody incorporated into his Wild West show, the relays thrilled audiences in Helena, Butte, Anaconda, and Missoula. The racers changed horses several times, riding each animal an equal distance. Sometimes they had to change their own saddles. Because the riders mounted and dismounted at high speed, the threat of spills and accidents kept tension—and interest—high.

In the summer of 1905, a Butte, Montana, show promoter contracted with Fannie and three other girls to ride relay races throughout the Midwest. Billed as the "Montana Girls," they were scheduled to perform in Butte before heading east. The day before the relay races, the manager of the Butte show talked Fannie into riding an "outlaw" bronc known as Tracy. Unfortunately, the local newspaper later reported, "she had about as much chance to ride Tracy as [boxer] Jim Jeffries would have of earning a decision in a bout with a circular saw." The horse bolted out of the chute, ran about 150 yards, and stopped dead, catapulting Fannie over his head. According to the *Butte Miner*,

. . . she made several revolutions in the air, and then struck the ground with a dull thud.

Women screamed, for it seemed that the frail equestrienne had been dashed to death. But Miss Sperry arose gamely, and approached the black demon, who had become entangled with the bridle reins, and was savagely pawing up the dirt in an effort to extricate himself. It was a rare exhibition of grit, and two thousand voices howled their approval.

Fannie had every intention of remounting the wild-eyed bronc, but men in the arena wouldn't allow it. Instead, they put a cowboy on the horse, and the show continued.

Fannie was one of only about a dozen women daring enough to ride bucking horses professionally just after the turn of the century. And she was one of only a tiny handful who rode "slick and clean," without hobbling the stirrups. Women bronc riders often tied their stirrups together with a cinch strap under the horse's belly, making it far more difficult to be thrown out of the saddle. Some considered it a less competitive way to ride. As Fannie put it, "it isn't giving the horse a fifty-fifty chance—fifty per cent in favor of him that he'll buck you off, fifty per cent in favor of you that you'll ride him." She also considered it too dangerous. With the stirrups hobbled, a rider couldn't kick free in time if a horse began to rear over backward, increasing the

chances that she would be crushed beneath it.

Fannie went on to win many accolades in her riding career. In 1912, the same year as her triumph at the Calgary Stampede, she teamed up with a partner—a thirty-four-year-old cowpuncher and part-time rodeo clown named Bill Steele. She met Bill while performing at a county fair in Deer Lodge, Montana, and she married him only a few months later, on April 30, 1912. They spent their honeymoon on the rodeo circuit.

It was in Sioux City, Iowa, during the second rodeo that the Steeles entered together, that Fannie received the most serious injuries of her career. Her steed stumbled, pinning her beneath it. "She arose from the ground immediately and stood uncertainly on her feet for a moment," the *Sioux City Journal* reported, "then fainted in the arms of her husband." A badly sprained back and hip kept her out of competition for several weeks. Yet, at her first show after her convalescence—a Frontier Days celebration in Winnipeg, Manitoba—she won her second women's world bucking horse championship.

What motivated Fannie to devote herself to so dangerous a sport? After all, she stood only five feet, seven inches tall, weighed about 120 pounds, and was described as "lithe, supple, and graceful." She once justified her obsession this way:

How can I explain to dainty, delicate women what it is like to climb down into a rodeo chute onto the back of a wild horse? How can I tell them it is a challenge that lies deep in the bones—a challenge that may go back to prehistoric man and his desire to conquer the wilderness . . . ? I have loved (bronc riding), every single, wonderful, suffering, exhilarating, damned, blessed moment of it. . . . Pain is not too great a price to pay for the freedom of the saddle and a horse between the legs.

In 1914, Bill and Fannie launched their own small Wild West show, touring towns and cities across Montana. During these performances, Fannie got a chance to show off her skills as a sharpshooter. With a rifle, she shattered china eggs that Bill held between his fingers and knocked the ash off cigars he clenched between his teeth. Once, when trying out a new rifle, she winged Bill in the finger. He simply used another to hold the egg, so the audience wouldn't notice the miss. When Fannie nicked that finger, too, blood gushed from Bill's hand, and they cut the act short. Bill must have been relieved to skip the cigar trick.

On another occasion, Bill was thrown from a horse, knocked unconscious, and presumed dead. The show promoter frantically cast about for someone to take his place for the rest of the program and found a willing substitute in Fannie. She later explained:

> *There wasn't even time for me to go to him, for I had to get ready to make his ride for him. That may seem callous, but we were show people in our own right, and "the show had to go on." I could lament for Bill later, but the horse had to be ridden right then.*

Fannie retired from professional riding in 1925. She and Bill—who had survived the fall—settled on a ranch near Helmville, Montana, where they worked as outfitters, guiding hunters into the backcountry. When Bill died in 1940, Fannie continued the small business alone for another twenty-five years. She died in Helena, Montana, on February 11, 1983, at the age of ninety-five, after having been inducted into both the National Cowboy and Cowgirl halls of fame.

"If there are not horses in heaven, I do not want to go there," she once said. "But I believe there will be horses in heaven as surely as God will be there, for God loved them or He would not have created them with such majesty."

Nancy Cooper Russell
(1878–1940)

Woman Behind the Man

ancy Cooper hustled around the steamy kitchen, helping "Ma" Roberts set the table and put the final touches on a special meal. Mr. Roberts was due home any minute, and he had sent word that he was bringing a dinner guest.

A jangle of spur rowels on the back porch signaled the arrival of the hungry pair. Ben Roberts breezed into the kitchen, followed by a sturdy cowboy who stopped short when he saw the pretty seventeen-year-old girl who had joined the Roberts household since his last visit. Mrs. Roberts introduced Nancy to their guest: Charlie Russell, former cowpuncher, fledgling artist, and close friend of the family. Nancy, she explained, had come to live with the Robertses in Cascade, Montana, to help care for their three children and do some of the housework.

Some say it was love at first sight. For the rest of the evening, Charlie was unusually gregarious, regaling his hosts with story after story of life in the good old days, when the West was still wild. Nancy was obviously enchanted. Thirty-four years after their introduction in October 1895, she described her first impression of this dashing maverick who would change her life:

The picture that is engraved on my memory of him is of a man a little above average height and weight, wearing a soft shirt, a Stetson hat on the back of his blonde head, tight trousers, held up by a "half-breed sash" that clung just above the hip bones, high-heeled riding boots on very small, arched feet. His face was Indian-like, square jaw and chin, large mouth, tightly closed firm lips, the under protruding slightly beyond the short upper, straight nose, high cheek bones, gray-blue deep-set eyes that seemed to see everything, but with an expression of honesty and understanding. . . . His hands were good-sized, perfectly shaped, with long, slender fingers. He loved jewelry and always wore three or four rings. . . . Everyone noticed his hands, but it was not the rings that attracted, but the artistic, sensitive hands that had great strength and charm. When he talked, he used them a lot to emphasize what he was saying, much as an Indian would do.

Charlie began spending a lot of time at the Roberts home, courting the sweet-faced, buxom lass whom everyone called Mamie. In the evenings, the pair would stroll along the bank of the Missouri River and out onto the wooden bridge that spanned it, talking and gazing at the fiery colors of the sunset reflected in the muddy current. Charlie proved just how captivated he was when he gave Nancy his beloved pinto, Monte.

Everyone warned the pair not to marry. The local doctor told Charlie that Nancy had frequent fainting spells—the sign, he said, of a bad heart. He predicted she'd be dead within three years. Folks reminded Nancy that Charlie had a drinking problem. On top of that, he was fourteen years older than she and a footloose bachelor who might well be set in his ways. And he'd never managed to make a decent living for himself. How could he ever be expected to provide for a family?

But, as Charlie might have said, love is as blind as a bear in a blizzard. He proposed to Nancy, an event later recounted by his nephew Austin Russell.

It took Charlie months to make up his mind, and when he finally asked Nancy she refused. He took her for a walk at sunset, they went down by the river and crossed the echoing, wooden bridge, and on the bridge he proposed, and she said No.

Years afterward, he made a little watercolor of it—an autumn evening, the sky darkening to night, a cold wind blowing and they have just left the bridge. Nancy, downcast, is walking in front with her hands in a muff, her coat buttoned up tight and a little black hat on her head. Charlie following close behind with his coat blown open and sash and white shirt showing . . . his arms extended in a pleading, persuading, arguing gesture, his hat on the back of his head. That's all there is to it; not much of a picture, but it tells the story.

In the end, of course, she said Yes.

Charlie and Nancy were married at twilight on September 9, 1896, in the parlor of the

Roberts home. Charlie had slicked himself up for the occasion, and Nancy wore a blue wedding gown that Mrs. Roberts had helped her make, along with a matching string of blue beads—her wedding gift from Charlie.

After the ceremony, the handful of guests celebrated with cake and ice cream while the newlyweds went on their "honeymoon." It was a short trip. The couple walked hand in hand about three hundred feet to the one-room shack that the

Roberts had loaned Charlie for a studio. Charlie had spent almost all the money he had fixing it up to be their first home. In fact, according to Austin Russell, the pair started their life together with only about seventy-five dollars between them.

Despite everyone's reservations, Mr. and Mrs. Charles M. Russell would stay devoted to each other for the next thirty years. And Nancy would have a profound impact on the course of Charlie's artistic career. Charlie himself later acknowledged in his own quaint fashion, "The lady I trotted in double harness with was the best booster an' pardner a man ever had. . . . If it hadn't been for Mamie I wouldn't have a roof over my head."

Today, some historians go even further. If the pair hadn't married, one of them contends, "it is doubtful that Russell would have created the prodigious body of artwork he did, a life's work that is truly one of our most cherished national treasures."

Nancy Cooper was born on May 4, 1878, in Mannsville, Kentucky, a town named for her great-great-grandfather. Her mother, Texas Annie Mann, had married young, which proved to be a disastrous mistake. Nancy's father, James Al Cooper, abandoned his pregnant wife within months of the wedding, so the mother-to-be moved back to her parents' home and resumed her maiden name.

AS A CHILD I
ALWAYS HAD A
FONDNESS FOR
ADVENTURE
AND OUTDOOR
EXERCISE
AND ESPECIAL
FONDNESS FOR
HORSES WHICH I
BEGAN TO RIDE
AT AN EARLY AGE
AND CONTINUED
TO DO SO UNTIL
I BECAME AN
EXPERT RIDER
BEING ABLE TO
RIDE THE MOST
VICIOUS AND
STUBBORN OF
HORSES, IN FACT
THE GREATER
PORTION OF MY
LIFE IN EARLY
TIMES WAS SPENT
IN THIS MANNER.

—Calamity Jane

As soon as Nancy could walk, she joined her mother and grandparents working in the family tobacco fields, plucking worms off the leafy plants. When she was five, she contracted diptheria, from which she barely recovered. For the rest of her life, her health would be fragile.

In 1884, Nancy's mother was married again, this time to her cousin James Thomas Allen, who had just come back to Kentucky after trying his hand at prospecting in Montana. Allen wanted no part of another man's child, so Nancy continued to live with her grandparents until her grandfather died and her step-grandmother went home to her family.

Nancy rejoined her mother in 1888, the same year her half-sister, Ella, was born. Two years later, Allen bundled his family onto a train and headed west to Helena, Montana, in search of a fortune in gold. When he had no luck finding a mining claim, he left his family behind and moved on to Idaho, dreaming of silver. He would send for them, he said, when he got established.

Life was hard for Texas Annie and her daughters with no one to provide for them. Mrs. Allen tried to earn a living with her sewing, while Nancy got a job doing domestic chores for fifty cents a day. One winter evening, she came home from work to find her mother in bed, burning with fever and coughing in fits. For the next nine months, she watched Texas Annie waste away until finally, when Nancy was sixteen, her once-lovely mother died of tuberculosis. Friends sent word to Allen, who returned to Helena just long enough to fetch Ella and take her back to Idaho. Nancy was left to fend for herself.

With the help of sympathetic friends, Nancy got a job with the Roberts family in Cascade, twenty-five miles southwest of Great Falls. They treated her so much like family that she called them Ma and Pa Roberts. Through them she met the most important man in her life.

About a year after their wedding, Nancy convinced Charlie to move to Great Falls, where there would be a bigger market for his paintings and sculptures. Charlie had quit the cowboy life and started trying to make a living as an artist only about three years earlier, and so far business was not exactly booming. A big part of the problem was Charlie's sociable nature. His buddies were always dropping in for a chat, or he was wandering over to the Mint or Silver Dollar Saloon for a friendly drink with the boys. He was too modest to ask people to buy his work—anyone who did was a "sucker." Instead, he gave many of his paintings away as gifts or used them as currency to pay his bills at the bars and grocery stores. Money was scarce, but Charlie was used to living on slim rations.

Nancy was more ambitious. She believed in her husband's talent and saw in it a ticket to prosperity. According to Russell biographer Harold McCracken,

> . . . *from the beginning she rode herd on him in an effort to keep him from spending too much time in the local saloon. . . . The bitter memories of her own parents' wrecked marriage had unquestionably left their mark—and a deep desire to find happiness and security for herself. . . .*
>
> *When [Charlie] was working on a picture and some of his former cronies dropped in for a visit or to invite him downtown for one-or-two [drinks], she refused to let them into the house or Charlie out. For this determined behavior, Nancy Russell was soon heartily disliked among some of the characters around Great Falls.*

Though Charlie no doubt missed these gab-fests with his friends, he conceded that Nancy had his best interests at heart. "If she hadn't prodded me," he said, "I wouldn't have done the work I did."

One day, Charles Schatzlein, a Butte store-keeper who had sold some of Charlie's pictures, stopped by the modest Russell home with a notion that would prove profitable for both Montana and American art. In *Good Medicine,* a collection of Charlie's letters that she edited after his death, Nancy recalled the man's advice:

"Do you know, Russell," he said, "you don't ask enough for your pictures. That last bunch you sent me, I sold one for enough to pay for six. I am paying you your price, but it's not enough. I think your wife should take hold of that end of the game and help you out."

From that time, the prices of Charlie's work began to advance until it was possible to live a little more comfortably.

Oddly enough, Nancy found that the higher she priced Charlie's paintings, the more people seemed to want them. Instead of the twenty-five dollars or so that Charlie had gotten for his oils, Nancy began asking—and getting—hundreds of dollars. Charlie admitted to his friends that he was embarrassed by Nancy's boldness and shocked when people paid the prices she asked. But he also had to admit that his reputation was growing. Schatzlein had judged correctly. Charlie had the soft heart, but Nancy had the head for business.

Eventually, Nancy realized that Montana was no place to make one's name and fortune as an artist. There simply weren't enough people there

who could afford to invest in art. So she began to wrangle exhibitions in some of the nation's major cities: first in Saint Louis, Charlie's hometown, then in Chicago and Denver, and finally in New York.

Though Charlie hated this place he called "the big camp" with "too many tepees," New Yorkers loved his realistic renderings of life among the cowboys and Indians of what was fast becoming the Old West. In 1911, Charlie exhibited at the prestigious Folsom Galleries in New York and in 1914 at the Dore Gallery in London. To Nancy's awe and delight, the Russells were soon dining with European nobility. They would never have to worry about money again.

By now the Russells had moved into a spacious two-story home in one of Great Falls' most respectable neighborhoods. Today, the white clapboard house on Fourth Avenue North is the nucleus of the C. M. Russell Museum complex. The Russells also built a lodge on spectacular Lake McDonald in Glacier National Park. They would spend almost every summer at this place, which they called Bull's Head Lodge for the symbol with which Charlie signed his art.

There was still one thing missing from the Russells' life, and Charlie especially felt the void. In 1916, when he was fifty-two and Nancy thirty-eight, they adopted an infant they named Jack.

Nancy was not an attentive mother. She often was out of town on business, and when she was home she seemed to have little patience with childish wants and needs. Much of the time, she left Jack in the care of friend and neighbor Josephine Trigg, though she tried to compensate by giving him all the material things she thought a boy could want. Charlie, on the other hand, doted on his son and, in Nancy's opinion, hopelessly spoiled him.

The Russells were now more prosperous than even Nancy had ever dreamed. But, according to author McCracken,

> . . . *success carried Charlie and his wife further and further apart in their respective conceptions of what were the most important things in life.* . . . *[T]he fruits of good fortune were much more appetizing to her than to him. Although Charlie's paintings were bringing prices running into five figures, she still rode herd on him with as unrelenting persistence as she had in the hungry days when they had first come to Great Falls.*

By now, Charlie had spent close to sixty years in the saddle, and he was nearing the end of the trail. Yet, even when he began to complain of feeling poorly, Nancy kept him at his easel. Soon Charlie was diagnosed with goiter, an enlargement of the thyroid gland, but he refused to undergo surgery. He wasn't about to let anyone "slit his throat," as he put it. When he finally consented to an operation at the Mayo Clinic in Rochester, Minnesota, it was too late. The goiter had already damaged his heart, and his doctor predicted he had three months to live. Charlie made the man promise not to tell Nancy, but she already knew—she had instructed the doctor to keep the bad news from Charlie. They went home pretending for each other's sake that all would be well.

On October 24, 1926, Charlie Russell died of a heart attack while checking on his sleeping ten-year-old son. Nancy devoted the rest of her life to promoting his work, even refusing two marriage proposals so that she could remain Mrs. Charles M. Russell. She moved to Pasadena, California, where she died on May 23, 1940, after suffering a stroke and developing bronchial pneumonia. She was buried by Charlie's side in Great Falls.

Cowboy actor William S. Hart, a longtime friend of the Russells, once offered a touching tribute to the couple's devotion: "One could never say Charlie without saying Nancy, too, for they were always together—a real man and a real woman."

Laura Gilpin
(1891–1979)

Cowgirl at Heart

Eighty-eight-year-old Laura Gilpin gripped her camera with aging but still steady hands, leaning as far as she could out of the small plane that carried her over the 250,000 acres of Navajo land that had become her adopted homeland. The tiny craft's wings dipped in the desert wind, seeming to almost lightly kiss the top branches of the piñon and cedar trees that dotted the landscape she had loved and photographed for nearly sixty years.

Laura had spent her life trying to capture and communicate the emotion of the deeply carved chasms of the Canyon De Chelly, the awesome limitlessness of the northern New Mexico desert, and the conquered but enduring nobility of the vanishing Rio Grande snaking its way tentatively southward, to "surrender its surplus to the sea." Laura Gilpin's photographs of the great Southwest helped others see through her eyes and understand what she considered the beating heart of the natural world, the timelessness of the terrain, and humanity's fleeting but inextricable connection to nature.

"In this great southwest," as Laura herself explains in her book, *The Pueblos: A Camera Chronicle,* "the vast landscape plays an all-important part in the lives of its people. Their architecture resembles the giant erosions of nature's carving. It is a land of contrasts, of gentleness and warmth, and fierce and raging storms; of timbered mountains and verdant valleys, and wide, arid desert; of gayety and song, and cruel strife."

Laura Gilpin got her first camera, a Kodak Brownie, as a present for her twelfth birthday. By age seventeen she was experimenting with autochrome and beginning to establish the very first cornerstones of her unique niche in the history of photography and of New Mexico. Laura was interested in the region as a maternal force that guided and defined the lives of the people who lived there. To her a photograph should not only document the land but also reflect its inner beauty. This idea was already a departure from the reality-based, male-dominated tradition of photography at that time.

Laura's male counterparts, such as Ansel Adams or such nineteenth-century photographer explorers as William Henry Jackson (to whom Laura was distantly related), photographed the West as a place of inviolate, pristine beauty, untouched by human habitation. For Laura the southwestern desert was not an unpolished jewel either awaiting or resisting the intrusion of human development, but a populated land rich with history and tradition inextricably bound up with the people who lived there. As Ansel Adams said after her death, she had "a highly individualistic eye. I don't have the sense that she was influenced except by the land itself."

Laura Gilpin's view of the landscapes she photographed take into account the human and emotional elements invoked by nature and, in so doing, have created a uniquely feminine vision of the terrain. Although she worked in a field traditionally dominated by men and in her own life insisted that her work was genderless, Gilpin's interpretations of the natural world, like some women writers of her day such as Willa Cather,

give a highly personal and human account of the landscape.

Despite her reputation as a "feminine" photographer, Laura Gilpin was intimately connected to the male tradition of western landscape photography. American landscape photography grew as a natural extension of the government survey teams that went west in the 1860s and 1870s to capture accurate images of the undeveloped American frontier. Photography was a physically challenging business in those days, not only because of the remoteness of the areas but because of the equipment the art required.

A person needed hundreds of pounds of equipment, gallons of chemicals and fresh water for development, and fragile glass-plate negatives to create a photograph. All of this had to be hauled up mountains and across vast, arid desert expanses in order to capture an image. It was a difficult and a lonely profession, requiring a good deal of grit and a thirst for adventure that was stronger than the need for human companionship. Most early explorer/photographers were spirited and independent men who were willing to spend many months away from their families and the comforts of home. A veteran of two decades of exploration photography, Carleton Watkins, complained to his wife in 1882, "I have never had the time seem so long to me on any trip I ever made from home, and I am not half done with my work. . . . It drags along awful slow, between the smoke and the rain and the wind, and as if the elements were not enough to worry me, a spark from an engine set fire to my . . . tent last week and burned it half up."

Survey photographers like Jackson or Watkins who photographed the West did not think of themselves as artists. They were surveyors, recording accurate photographic data that reflected what their government and railroad employers wanted to see: an expansive and inviting new land, unpopulated, and welcoming commercial development. Although these photographers made pictures of great beauty, their chief purpose was to document the land in the interests of American settlement.

All of this isolation and backbreaking enterprise would have seemed a strange path indeed for a young woman of Laura's generation to choose. But Laura was not an average young woman. Laura Gilpin grew up appreciating the rough and ready splendor of the West, and throughout her life remained a cowgirl at heart. She could camp out in the woods for days on end or lean out of an airplane at eighty-eight years of age if it meant

getting the picture that she wanted. And she was a woman who could tolerate solitude. Laura worked for most of her life in virtual isolation, waiting in the silent, remote regions of the Southwest to hear the desert whisper its secrets to her.

Laura Gilpin was born in 1891 just outside Colorado Springs. She was distantly related to William Gilpin, the visionary expansionist and explorer who became Colorado's first territorial governor, and to the photographer William Henry Jackson. So she had, embedded in her genealogical history, the combination of pioneer and photographer that would steer her course.

As a girl, she knew Dr. William A. Bell, who had photographed along the thirty-second parallel for the Kansas Pacific Railroad in 1867. She was also a friend of General William Jackson Palmer, founder of the Denver and Rio Grande Railroad and to whom she herself accredited her lifelong love affair with the geography of the West.

Laura Gilpin's father, Frank, was a scion of Baltimore society with a misplaced love of the open range. He, like a lot of young men of his generation, went west, moving to Colorado in 1880 to seek his fortune. He tried his hand at ranching, mining, and investing before settling down to a career as a fine furniture maker in the late 1920s.

Laura's mother, Emma Miller Gilpin, did not share her husband's enthusiasm for the unwashed and, as far as she was concerned, uncivilized Southwest. Emma was from a prominent St. Louis family, and although she followed her husband west, she always tried to bring her love of Eastern refinement and culture into the family's rustic homelife. She encouraged Laura to study music and art and insisted that her daughter be educated at the finest East Coast boarding schools. But Laura, who was much more in tune with her father's wide-ranging sensibilities, felt out of place in the traditional Eastern boarding-school setting that backdropped her life from 1905 until 1909, and she was rumored to have asserted her unique spirit by showing up at cotillions in cowboy outfits. Eventually she was allowed to come back to the West that she loved.

In 1916, after experimenting with photography for more than a decade, Laura Gilpin left the West once more and moved to New York to study photographic pictorialism at the Clarence H. White School. Rather like the impressionists' influence upon painting as a medium, pictorialists emphasized feeling and emotion rather than accurate physical description. Pictorialism was characterized by soft-focus-lens views of a hazy, romanticized world that appealed to Laura, and negatives and prints were manipulated to produce a more atmospheric and evocative image. They were an important step away from the work of survey photographers and toward a more artistic vision of photography.

Laura returned to the Southwest a year later, profoundly influenced by White's pictorial style. Her own creative inclinations had been radicalized by White's idea of photography as an art form. Years after, Laura recalled White's influence on her: "Many enter the field of photography with the impulse to record a scene. They often fail to realize that what they wish to do is to record the emotion felt upon viewing that scene. . . . a mere record photograph in no way reflects that emotion."

Shortly after her return to Colorado, Laura opened a commercial studio specializing in portraiture and began taking pictures of the nearby mountains and prairies of eastern Colorado.

Her work won some early accolades in the press, most notably her picture of the Colorado prairie, which New York critics praised as giving "most successfully the sense of the vastness of the plains." Whereas a single tree or outcropping might represent an entire mountain range for documentary photographers, Laura focused on the big picture. Laura wanted to suggest the vast and mythic expanse of the place—the majestic scale of nature—so that she could better suggest the sweep of human history and the impact of the environment on patterns of human settlement.

Guided by this vision, in the 1920s Laura became increasingly interested in the rich historical legacy of the Southwest. She made her first trip to Mesa Verde in 1924 and tried to express through her photographs the tentative but enduring culture of the ancient cliff dwellers. The spare simplicity of their lives intrigued Laura, and the pictures she took at this time were soft-focus, evocative images that suggested the romantic spirit of the place.

As Martha Sandweiss, in her essay "Laura Gilpin and the Tradition of American Landscape Photography," explains it:

Gilpin's broad, emotional response to Mesa Verde [she returned in 1925] was much like that of Willa Cather, whose story about the discovery of the ruins, The Professor's House, *came out in 1925. Cather's hero, Tom Outland, lamented the fact that "we had only a small Kodak, and these pictures didn't make much show—looked, indeed, like scrubby little 'dobe ruins such as one can find almost anywhere. They gave no idea of the beauty and vastness of the setting." Gilpin thought her pictures of the majestic, sculptural ruins compensated for Outland's shortcomings. Some of Cather's writings even seemed to describe her own photographs. "Far above me," Cather had written, "a thousand feet or so, set in a great cavern in the face of the cliff, I saw a little city of stone, asleep. It was still as sculpture—and something like that. It all hung together, seemed to have a kind of composition." Gilpin hoped to interest Cather in collaborating on an illustrated edition of* The Professor's House; *unfortunately, her efforts to contact the author failed.*

Laura Gilpin self-published her Mesa Verde photographs in 1927 in the book The Mesa Verde National Park: Reproductions from a Series of Photographs *by Laura Gilpin.*

Laura first encountered the subject that was to dominate the rest of her artistic life in 1930. While driving on the Navajo Indian reservation in remote southwestern New Mexico with her friend Elizabeth Forster, Laura ran out of gas. Laura, always a sturdy traveler, hiked more than 10 miles to the nearest trading post to get more fuel. When she returned, she found her friend playing rummy with a group of Navajo Indians who had arrived to keep her company. A lifelong kinship between Laura and the Navajos was born in that moment, and throughout the rest of her life, Laura photographed the Navajos, lovingly creating an intelligent and compassionate record of a beleaguered Pueblo culture.

In 1930 she was elected an associate of the Royal Photographic Society of Great Britain, and in that same year the Library of Congress purchased a small collection of her photographs, but the Depression threatened the survival of her tiny gallery, and she was forced to focus on earning money. Laura published her own postcards and lantern slides and, in 1941, her first major book, *The Pueblos: A Camera Chronicle.* In the text of this book, Gilpin expressed her reverence for the ancient history of the Southwest, which was as "old as Egypt." Laura felt a connection with the rich history of the Pueblo and claimed it as her own. "There is something infinitely appealing in this land which contains our oldest history," she wrote, "something which once known will linger in one's memory with a haunting tenacity."

The photographs were a critical but not a financial success, and so, during the Second World War, Laura worked part-time as a photographer for Boeing to make ends meet. After the war she resettled in Santa Fe. In 1948 she published *Temples in the Yucatán: A Camera Chronicle of Chichen Itza.*

Laura's next book, *The Rio Grande: River of Destiny,* published in 1949, introduced a more mature and self-confident Laura Gilpin to the world. She placed a much greater emphasis, in

this book, on cultural geography, a theme that was to also dominate the rest of her creative life.

Laura began work on the Rio Grande book in 1945, and during the next four years, she traveled more than 27,000 miles on borrowed gas ration coupons to make photographs for this ambitious project. Because the region was largely inaccessible by car, Laura packed in on horseback to photograph the river's source in Colorado, and she chartered a small plane to fly her over the river's confluence with the Gulf of Mexico. Author Martha Sandweiss describes Laura's book this way:

> *Her plan for the book dictated the content of her pictures: The people—the Spanish Americans, the Mexicans and the Anglos are important but are subservient to the river. The people come and go—the river flows on forever. Thus she made few portraits, focusing instead on landscapes and pictures that showed the people in the context of their environment. She organized the book geographically, following the river down through the Colorado mountains and the fertile San Luis Valley, into the Indian and Hispanic regions of northern New Mexico, and out through the ranching areas of west Texas and the Mexican borderlands.*

John Brinkerhoff Jackson, himself a student of the American landscape, reviewed the book as a "human geographical study," noting that Gilpin,

> *. . . has seen the river from its source to its end and permits us to see it through her eyes, not merely as a photogenic natural phenomenon, but as a force that has created a whole pattern of living, that has created farms and villages and towns and that continues to foster their growth. . . . Miss Gilpin is undoubtedly the first photographer to introduce us to the pueblos, the Spanish-American communities, the whole countryside of farms, as something more than picturesque.*

Laura's interest in cultural context, though less prominent in her photographs, was now expressed in text. She lovingly describes the region in human terms, citing the river's mineral wealth, its use in growing food and nurturing livestock, and its value as an oasis for weary travelers looking for a place to settle.

The final page of the book, featuring a picture called "Rio Grande Yields Its Surplus to the Sea (1947)," makes an evocative statement, in text and image, about Laura Gilpin's feelings regarding the beauty and fragility of the relationship between humanity and the natural world. The text reads:

Since the earliest-known existence of human life in the Western world, all manner of men have trod the river's banks. With his progressing knowledge and experience, man has turned these life-giving waters upon the soil, magically evoking an increasing bounty from the arid land. But through misuse of its vast drainage area—the denuding of forest lands and the destruction of soil-binding grasses—the volume of the river has been diminished, as once generous tributaries have become parched arroyos. Will present

and future generations have the vision and wisdom to correct these abuses, protect this heritage, and permit a mighty river to fulfill its highest destiny?

Almost immediately upon finishing *The Rio Grande: River of Destiny,* Laura returned to the Navajo reservation with Elizabeth Forster, resolved to do another book on Navajo life. This time she wanted to emphasize Navajo tradition and cultural continuity, so she rephotographed many of the people that she had photographed years before, paying special attention to those who had preserved their ancient culture. She organized her book into four sections, corresponding to the importance of the number four in the Navajo religion. Laura wanted the book, which would be called *The Enduring Navaho,* to be written and photographed from a purely Navajo perspective.

The Navajo considered themselves the Dinéh, "the People of the Earth." As Laura wrote,

. . . they moved about in loneliness, though never lonely, in dignity and happiness, with song in their heart and on their lips, in harmony with the great forces of nature.

The two salient qualities of the people were their dignity and their happiness. Both spring from their vital traditional faith, faith in nature, faith in themselves as a part of nature, faith in their place in the universe, deep-rooted faith born of their Oriental origin, molded and strengthened by the land in which they live.

The most important theme at work in *The Enduring Navaho* is the word enduring. Laura, like Elsie Clews Parsons, believed that Pueblo culture was alive and thriving in constant combination with new influences—remaining connected to the past, yet moving forward.

In 1972 Laura Gilpin published a book on the Canyon de Chelly. She was eighty-one years old. In this book she closely followed the lives of a small number of Navajo families that live in this New Mexico canyon, which is accessible only on horseback, led by a Navajo guide.

Laura Gilpin created a pictorial portrait of the entire historical and geological landscape of the Southwest. As Martha Sandweiss put it, Gilpin communicated

. . . a landscape with a past measured not just in geological or evolutionary time but in human time, as evidenced by architectural ruins, ancient trails, and living settlements. It was a landscape with intrinsic beauty, but one whose greatest meaning derived from its potential to change and be changed by humankind. Gilpin did not dislike the idea of a wilderness, but for her there was no true wilderness in the Southwest, no area that had remained untouched by more than a thousand years of human settlement.

Laura never considered herself an artist. She was simply a photographer, who, for more than a half a century, practiced her profession with consummate craftsmanship and a great love for the world she captured with her camera.

Laura Gilpin knew that the Southwest sometimes provided a nurturing landscape, sometimes a hostile one. She knew that the landscape could be modified by human action, but she also believed that the landscape should and would remain the dominant force shaping and molding human culture.

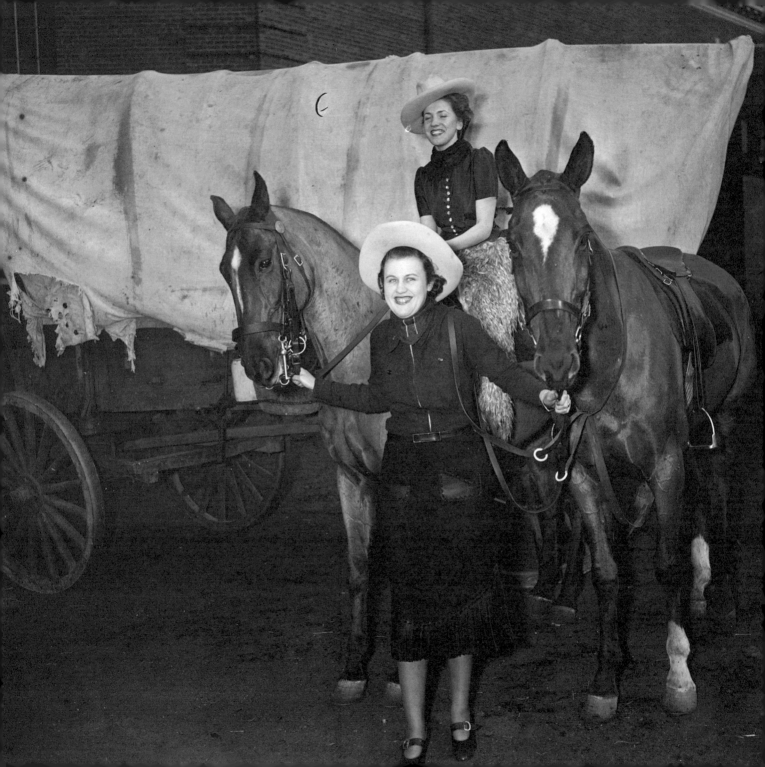

Pearl Hart

(1871–?)

Arizona's Lady Bandit

According to one story, it was a hot and windy Tucson day in 1928 when a taxi pulled up outside the Pima County Jail. A diminutive woman, somewhere in her mid- to late fifties, stepped out. She was neatly dressed in a freshly ironed skirt and blouse and paused to speak quietly to the driver before walking to the prison entrance.

The prison attendant asked if he could help her, and she responded, "I want to look over your jail, and I'd like to see my old cell. I'm Pearl Hart."

Surprised but compliant, the young man guided her around the facility. When they came to her cell, she stepped in, paused, then touched the walls gently. A couple of tears slid down one wrinkled cheek. She turned and slowly walked out of the jail and back to the waiting taxi.

She was never heard from again.

It's a touching story, but like so many others about Pearl Hart, firm evidence of its veracity is hard to come by.

By the 1890s the Indians had been relocated to reservations, the buffalo herds had been slaughtered, and the real Wild West had vanished, leaving a mythical one in its place. Popular magazines such as *Harper's, Atlantic,* and *Scribner's* were filled with nostalgic western fiction by Owen Wister and Zane Grey, and in 1893 alone, Buffalo Bill's Wild West Show was seen by six million people and took in $1 million.

So it was that on a hot June day in 1899, a petite woman named Pearl Hart was apprehended for holding up a stagecoach. And the idea of a female stagecoach robber snared the imagination of the country. In a nineteenth-century version of a media circus, journalists swarmed the trial and the prison where Pearl was held. Almost no aspect of her life can be verified for certain, and as an enthusiastic spinner of tales, Pearl herself contributed mightily to the wealth of stories. One writer, describing her stint as a miners' cook, wrote that she was "a good cook, an extremely pretty girl, and virtuous, firmly resisting the advances of the men in that boisterous camp. Her salary was generous, but most of it went to helping others."

Yet, according to another account: "She peddled her earthly charm and sparse physical attraction to the non-discriminating desires of the miners. Her abject lifestyle led to an early narcotics addiction and suggested contraction of venereal disease." She was often described as being a cigar smoker, and one contemporary journalist described her as a "hop fiend of insatiable appetite."

Most agree that Pearl Taylor was born in Canada, in Lindsay, Ontario, in 1871. Her parents were well-to-do and religious and made sure their daughter was educated at the best schools available.

According to her own account, when she was sixteen and still in boarding school, she fell in love with a hard-living gambler named Frank Hart. He convinced her to elope, and she soon discovered that marrying him was a disastrous idea. The gambling was bad enough—but not as painful as the physical abuse. She tried leaving him, but like many battered wives, she went back to him and to the same old pattern repeatedly, hoping he'd improve.

In Chicago, during the closing of the 1893 World's Fair, she left him a second time, perhaps in the company of a piano player named Dan Bandman, and went by train to Trinidad, Colorado. In an interview with *Cosmopolitan* years later, she told the interviewer: "I was only twenty-two years old. I was good-looking, desperate, discouraged, and ready for anything that might come. I do not care to dwell on this period of my life. It is sufficient to say that I went from one city to another until some time later I arrived in Phoenix."

Depending on which biographer one reads, she supported herself by singing, cooking—or by freelancing in the world's oldest profession.

Frank tracked her down, and she returned to him again. Life was good for three years. She'd had a son during their first year of marriage, and a daughter was born while they all lived in Phoenix. Frank wasn't the only one living the uninhibited life: Word had it that Pearl was a heavy smoker and drinker, as well as a morphine user.

When the abuse started again, she sent the children to her mother in Toledo, Ohio, and left for a third time. No record of the two children remains.

In 1898 Frank found her again and convinced her to move to Tucson. "After the money I had saved had been spent, he began beating me, and I lived in hell for months," she told *Cosmopolitan.* Finally, he joined Teddy Roosevelt's Rough Riders regiment and went off to the Spanish-American War. Pearl never saw him again.

She drifted back to Phoenix, depressed and discouraged—to the point of trying to kill herself three or four times. Each time, she said, friends or acquaintances succeeded in stopping her.

In 1899 Pearl finally found a job in a boardinghouse cooking for miners in Mammoth, on the San Pedro River, almost halfway between Globe and Tucson. The work was hard, and she lived in a soggy tent on the edge of the Gila River.

About this time, she met a miner named Joe Boot, a handsome dark-haired man with a New England accent and an opulent handlebar moustache. He agreed with Pearl that life had to be easier in Globe, but the impediment was getting there: Three mountain ranges lay between the two towns, and the road, which turned to clay soup during rain, was narrow and nearly impassible at the best of times.

After several days of slogging through the mud, they eventually arrived in Globe, where Pearl found another boardinghouse job. But her streak of bad luck continued. One of the big local mines closed, and she was once again without work.

"On top of all my other troubles," she later told *Cosmopolitan,* "I got a letter just at this time saying my mother was dying and asking me to come home if I wanted to see her alive again. That letter drove me crazy. No matter what I had been, my mother had been my dearest, truest friend, and I longed to see her alive again. From what I know now, I believe I became temporarily insane."

Joe Boot invited her to help him work an old mining claim he had, and the two spent grueling days heaving picks and shovels—in vain. They struck no gold.

Who knows which of them suggested robbing the Globe stagecoach, but the idea seemed like a good one. The route was one of the last stagecoach runs in the territory, and because it hadn't been held up in years, no shotgun rider rode along, just the driver, a cheerful man named Henry Bacon. The coach usually held a load of "drummers"— salesmen—who more than likely carried full purses.

On a summer day in 1899, as the stage pulled up at a watering hole near Cane Springs Canyon, just south of the Dripping Springs Mountains, the robbery unfolded. Bacon stopped to let the horses drink and to allow the passengers a chance to stretch their legs after the jolting 30-mile trip.

Before they had a chance to do so, two bandits appeared. Even on horseback, one was obviously much taller than the other.

As Pearl reported in *Cosmopolitan*, Joe commanded the passengers and driver out of the stage and told them to "Throw up your hands!" while she, clad in a rough shirt, blue overalls, a mask, dirty cowboy hat, and boots that were too big, covered them with her .38. She dismounted and searched the stage, finding two guns.

"Really," she was reported to have commented later, "I can't see why men carry revolvers because they invariably give them up at the very time they were made to be used."

Next, she searched the men:

I found on the fellow who was shaking the worst three hundred and ninety dollars. This fellow was trembling so I could hardly get my hand in his pockets. The other fellow, a sort of a dude, with his hair parted in the middle, tried to tell me how much he needed the money, but he yielded thirty-six dollars, a dime and two nickels. Then I searched the remaining passenger, a Chinaman. He was nearer my size and I just scared him to death.

"Cow Girls" at the

His clothes enabled me to go through him quickly. I only got five dollars, however.

Kindhearted robbers that they were, Pearl and Joe made sure each passenger had a dollar so he'd have money to buy dinner. She kept the driver's .45—a costly souvenir, as it later turned out—and the two bandits hightailed it for the hills. As soon as they were out of sight, Bacon unhitched one of the horses and galloped back to Globe, where he alerted the sheriff.

Once again, accounts vary wildly about the events of the next few days. Some say the pair were so unprepared and disorganized that they had neither an escape plan nor horses nor even spare water. The duo bumbled about in the desert, circling until they inadvertently walked into the sheriff's hands.

According to Pearl, the two began a wild ride in, out, and across steep canyons and rugged desert country in an effort to confuse the officers. "I marvel that we did not lose our lives," she said later. They camped that night and the next day near Riverside.

The second night they rode hard, aiming for Benson and the railroad. Somewhere near Mammoth, they clambered "up a sandstone hill where there were many small caves, or holes, of a circular shape, not much larger than a man's body. Upon reaching this spot of safety we found it to be the home of wild or musk hogs [probably javelinas]. . . . However our peril was so great that we could not hesitate about

TON "ROUND UP" 1911

official Photo
copyright 1911 by
Marcell
at Portland

other chances, and we selected a hole into which we could crawl. Joe started in and I followed. Of course, we had to look out for rattlesnakes, too, which made our entrance very slow."

Joe shot the hog, and the pair hid out that night and the next day. Again, they rode all night, then stopped to rest just after daylight.

"After this we lay down but were destined not to sleep long. About three hours after lying down, we were awakened by yelling and shooting. We sprang up and grabbed our guns, but found we were looking straight into the mouths of two gaping Winchesters in the hands of the sheriff's posse."

They were within 20 miles of the Benson railroad station, and Pearl always believed that if they had reached the station and caught the train, they'd have escaped.

The posse was headed by Pinal County Sheriff William Truman, who on June 4, 1899, escorted the two by train to Casa Grande, then by buckboard to Florence. That jail lacked facilities for women prisoners, so Pearl was transferred to Tucson. Although some accounts have her claiming that she "would never consent to be tried under

a law she or her sex had no voice in making, or to which a woman had no power under the law to give her consent," no evidence exists to show that Pearl was ever a supporter of women's suffrage.

The first trial jury (of twelve men) listened to Pearl who, according to some reports, wept, wrung her hands, flipped her frilly skirts, and batted her eyelashes. They handed down a "not guilty" verdict, which infuriated Judge Fletcher M. Doan. He sent Pearl and Joe back to Tucson to await a federal trial on new charges of interfering with the mail.

Reactions varied. Some admired the spunky little woman, while others worried what her actions had done to the already fragile status of women. The editorial writer of the Yuma paper, the *Arizona Sentinel,* went on record to say that:

> . . . *the acquittal of a female stage robber who had acknowledged her guilt in writing is not likely to do the woman much good, as she was immediately rearrested. . . . The action, which will be telegraphed all over the country, is, however, likely to do the reputation of Arizona a considerable amount of injury, as it will confirm many eastern people in the idea that the people of Arizona have a sneaking sympathy for such*

crimes. . . . In these days of woman's rights, the question of sex should not be allowed to play any greater part in crime that it is supposed to do in merit and achievement.

On October 12, 1899, Pearl enlisted the help of a trusty, an inmate possibly named Ed Hogan, who helped cut a hole in her cell wall. The two of them then walked down the stairs to a couple of waiting horses, rode to the railroad tracks, and hopped an eastbound freight train. U.S. Marshal George Scarborough apprehended them in Deming, New Mexico, and Pearl was returned to Florence. Ironically, Scarborough had recognized her from the photographs in the *Cosmopolitan* article that had come out several days earlier.

The second trial was held in November, and the jury (one account has it made up of mostly women) found the pair guilty of stealing the stagecoach driver's pistol, which was worth a whopping $10. Joe was sentenced to thirty years for highway robbery in Yuma's Arizona Territorial Prison—a jail with a reputation for being impossible to escape. The officers there were obviously unimpressed by Joe and described him as a "weak, morphine-depraved specimen of male mortality, without spirit and lacking intelligence and activity. It is plain that the woman was the leader of this partnership."

Pearl was assigned No. 1559 and was sentenced to five years in the same jail. According to her prison record, she was Catholic, married with two children, and a woman of "Intemperate" habits, addicted to both tobacco and morphine. She was five feet three inches tall, weighed one hundred pounds, and claimed a shoe size of two and a half. Her eyes were listed as gray: her hair, black.

She is said to have spent much of her time making lace items to sell to prison visitors. Although some accounts describe Pearl as almost illiterate, the prison record lists her as being able to read and write. In addition, seven months after her incarceration, a reporter for the *Arizona Sentinel* wrote: "Pearl Hart's cussedness is manifesting itself in a more alarming direction than holding up stages. She has taken to writing poetry and is unwinding it by the yard."

She certainly had no shortage of salty vocabulary. At one point she said she was lonely and wanted the prison dog, Judie, and her fox terrier puppies to play in the space assigned as her "yard." The owner, the prison's assistant superintendent, Ira Smith, is reputed to have refused her request because "Judie is a lady, and her pups are well-bred and he doesn't propose to have their morals contaminated by Pearl. Any horse thief or Mexican murderer can fondle the pups, but Ira draws the line at Pearl."

She did at least have some human company. A photograph taken in 1902 shows Pearl accompanied by two women, fellow inmates Elena Estrada and Rosa Duran, in the female ward. The facility, made from some steel cages and an old guardhouse, was a two-story structure, consisting of two cells upstairs and an open room below. According to U.S. Department of the Interior records, the prison still had no matrons or female officers, although the board had voted to hire a matron in 1897, at half the salary of a male guard.

By 1901 Pearl's comrade in crime, Joe, had worked his way up the prison employment ladder and had earned a position as the warden's personal cook. On February 6, he quietly walked out the prison gates, never to be heard from again.

On December 15, 1902, the country was mighty surprised to hear that as of that date, Pearl Hart would be a free woman, despite having two years to go of her sentence. The governor, Alexander O. Brodie, refused to comment, and the reason for her abrupt release remained a secret for fifty years. In 1954 George Smalley, the governor's secretary, revealed that Pearl had become pregnant in jail. Only three men had been allowed to visit without supervision—and one of them was the governor himself.

RANCH WOMEN ARE AS SHARP AS NAILS AND JUST AS HARD. IF EVE HAD BEEN A RANCH WOMAN, SHE WOULD NEVER HAVE TEMPTED ADAM WITH AN APPLE. SHE WOULD HAVE ORDERED HIM TO MAKE HIS MEAL HIMSELF.

—Anthony Trollope, 1862

There's no proof that she was truly pregnant, and no record of a birth.

But the fact remains that, attired in a new dress and hat, and clutching a first-class ticket to Kansas City, all courtesy of the Territory of Arizona, Pearl left Yuma. One story says she was the star of a three-act morality play written by her sister. Another says she performed in various Wild West shows before being arrested as Mrs. L. P. Keele in Kansas City for stealing canned goods or leading a gang of pickpockets—or both. Yet another version describes her as leading a dreary, lonely life and waiting tables in a Los Angeles hash house.

Most common and most reliable is the account of Pearl eventually marrying a cowboy miner named Calvin Bywater and moving to a ranch near Globe. There she's said to have lived well into her nineties, living the quiet life of a hardworking, stout ranch woman.

Jane Candia Coleman, author of a partly fictionalized biography *I, Pearl Hart,* recalls seeing a now-vanished journal.

The diary was just about her day-to-day life in Globe. It was a dull account: "Today we bought groceries." "Today we planted a tree." The journal was that of a boring old lady who eradicated all evidence of her earlier life. She was freely literate— not uneducated and not a fool. She had nice handwriting. It was a boring account, keeping her secrets.

Mrs. Clarence Woody, a Gila County historian who had worked as the local census taker, remembered in a 1974 interview counting Pearl Bywater in 1940 and again when she worked the agricultural census in 1948. She and several other local old-timers said they also recalled seeing Pearl in Globe in 1957, which would have made her eighty-six years old.

Mrs. Woody, eighty-nine at the time of the interview, also remembered asking Pearl where she was from. The answer was brusque.

"I wasn't born anywhere."

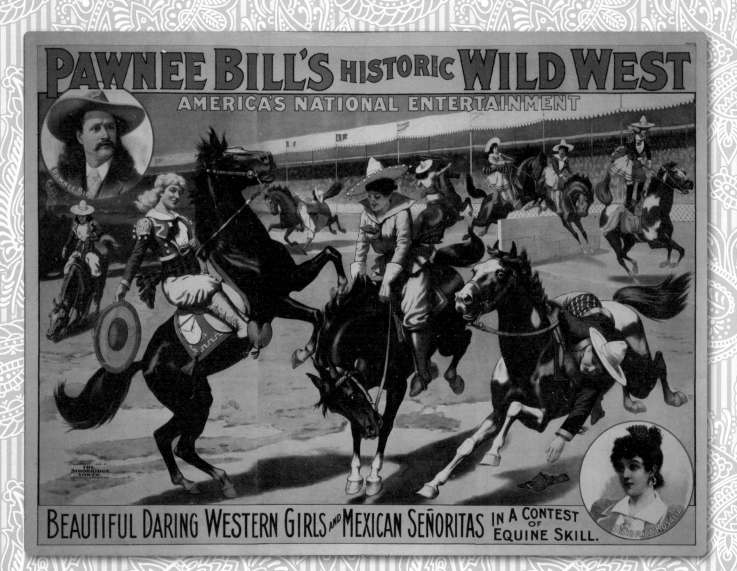

Mary Kidder Rak

(1879–1958)

Rancher and Writer

Mary sat against the adobe wall of the cabin, savoring the balmy November day and the solitude. Robles, a shepherd mix, lay at her feet, seeming to enjoy the peace as much as his mistress was.

Mary's husband, Charlie, was away for ten days hauling steers to Los Angeles—an arduous trip from their 22,000-acre ranch high in the Chiricahua Mountains of southeastern Arizona.

This wasn't the first time Charlie had left Mary alone at the ranch, and she always relished the respite. Except for thirty steers by the barn, all the horses and cattle were out on the range where browse was plentiful. Mary was happy for the unaccustomed hours of rest between morning and evening feeding.

"Basking in the sun, sometimes I sat and thought, sometimes I just sat," she wrote later in *A Cowman's Wife*.

And, besides, if any emergency did occur, she secretly considered herself completely capable of handling any situation that might arise.

The capricious weather of the Chiricahuas almost proved her wrong.

"Charlie, I am sure, would have recognized the unseasonably warm days for what they were, weather-breeders; but I was entirely unprepared for what was to come," she wrote.

The next morning, Mary awoke to a cloudy, oppressive day, and she used her time to fill the coal-oil lamps, gather wood for the fireplace and kitchen stove, and to bring in extra food from the storeroom. She always had a month's worth of supplies on hand because going to town was no easy jaunt for local ranchers in the 1930s. The nearest town was Douglas, five hours and 56 bone-jolting miles away.

As an afterthought, she made one more trip to the barn and returned with a shovel.

In mid-afternoon, as the temperature

plummeted, occasional flakes of snow wafted toward the dusty brown earth. Just in case of an approaching storm, she fed the steers an hour earlier than usual. By the time she'd finished, the wind was snatching the hay from the pitchfork, and she could "no longer see the near-by peaks, so thick was the falling snow. Falling is not quite the right term for it, either. Snow seemed to fill the air, coming from every direction at once. Even after it had reached the ground, whirling gusts seized upon the snow and bore it aloft, juggling the flakes in the air."

The chickens became so hysterical Mary had to catch and carry them, one by one, to the hen house before retreating to the cabin with Robles.

All night the snow continued, and the wind howled as it uprooted trees, which dragged the telephone line down as they fell.

When Mary rose the next morning, the storm had abated, but drifts jammed the doorways, and the thermometer revealed a most unusual temperature: five degrees below zero. She forced her way out the door and, grateful that she'd retrieved the shovel, she dug paths to the barn and then more paths to the feeding troughs for the cattle. No sooner had she wearily finished than the wind gathered strength again, and yet another snowstorm roared up the canyon.

By the third day the horses made their way down the mountain to the barn, hoping for grain because snow had buried all the grass, adding more mouths to feed. Again she shoveled out paths, again she fed the hungry livestock and chickens.

Five days after the storm, the paths around the ranch remained clear, but Mary "heard a sound that made my heart drop down into my rubber boots. Snow, melting on vast slopes, had reached the river, which now would roar down the canyon for days, fed from huge drifts on the high mountains above us." The road to Old Camp Rucker Ranch crossed the now-impassable White River five times. It would be days before anyone could drive in.

In the meantime Charlie had read the news about heavy snows in southern Arizona and had returned from California. He'd arranged to meet one of their neighbors in Douglas for a ride home, but the man didn't get far from his own ranch before becoming stuck in a snow drift. Charlie was able to catch a ride to the southern end of the Chiricahua range, and then he walked 4 miles to another ranch, where he borrowed a horse and saddle.

Then, according to Mary, "he rode home through twelve miles of deep snow, over fallen logs and under snow-laden branches."

Her reaction to his unexpected appearance at the door?

"I wonder if real pioneer women ever cried for joy?"

Mary Kidder Rak may not have considered herself a real pioneer woman, but she certainly worked as hard as any western settler. Like many other early 1900s ranch women, she was originally a city dweller and came to ranching late in life.

Pioneering, determination, and an itch to travel seem to have run in her family. Three of her ancestors came to America on the Mayflower, two were colonial governors, and five fought for the colonies in the American Revolution.

Mary's father, Ichabod Norton Kidder, was an attorney who was born in Edgartown, Massachusetts. In 1867, at the age of twenty-nine, his residence was listed as Boonesboro, Iowa, but when he married nineteen-year-old Eliza Allen Luce, it was in Tisbury, Massachusetts, on Martha's Vineyard. Twelve years later, Mary was born in Boone, Iowa, on August 4, 1879. No records have survived of Mary's childhood, but she apparently did spend some time on Martha's Vineyard with her mother's family.

In 1893 the Kidders moved to California, and Mary attended Troop Polytechnic Institute in Pasadena until 1896. According to one source, she aspired to a stage career but was persuaded by her family to attend college instead.

She attended Stanford University, and in 1901 she received a bachelor's degree in history. For several years she taught public school in San Francisco. From 1905 to 1917 she was a social worker in an organization called the Associated Charities, the first general, nonsectarian relief organization in the area (now the Family Service Agency of San Francisco).

WHAT WE WANT TO DO IS GIVE OUR WOMEN EVEN MORE LIBERTY THAN THEY HAVE. LET THEM DO ANY KIND OF WORK THAT THEY SEE FIT, AND IF THEY DO IT AS WELL AS MEN, GIVE THEM THE SAME PAY.

—William F. "Buffalo Bill" Cody, 1899

In 1906 disaster struck the city. At 5:13 A.M., April 18, an earthquake shook the West from Coos Bay, Oregon, to Los Angeles, and east to central Nevada. Fires blazed throughout San Francisco for four days straight, and vast tenements collapsed as the ground melted beneath their foundations. Three thousand people died, and the damage was estimated at $500 million.

The Associated Charities directed earthquake relief for the city, and the following year it established an employment bureau to help during the economic depression brought on by the earthquake and fire.

During the next few years, the group also set up a Department of Unmarried Mothers and Their Babies, which allowed the closing of "foundling asylums" and led to improved foster care and adoption programs. Sometime during this period, Mary became superintendent of the Associated Charities.

Like Mary Kidder, Charles Lukeman Rak, a cowpuncher from New Mexico and Texas, had also moved to California. The two met while he was in school at Berkeley studying forestry. They were married March 30, 1917, and soon moved to Tucson, where Mary taught at the University of Arizona, and Charlie worked for the state forest service.

It wasn't long before she put her social service experience to work. In 1919 she sent questionnaires covering forty-eight topics, including "The Care of the Feeble-minded," child welfare, use of school buildings for recreational and social purposes, county jails, and "Homes for Aged and Infirm Arizona Pioneers," to every philanthropic and service agency in the state.

Based on the responses, she compiled A Social Survey of Arizona. In the introduction she wrote as follows: "It is earnestly hoped that the splendid flood of social service enthusiasm, which had its source in devoted war work, will be diverted into peace channels and find some guidance in this little Survey." She was unafraid to express her own opinion:

A county jail is an unpleasant place which we would all prefer comfortably to ignore, but since its unwilling inmates will sooner or later be free to mingle with their fellows on the outside, it is of the greatest importance to all of us that they come forth in better physical, mental and more condition than when their imprisonment began.

It is earnestly hoped that those who read this bulletin will be willing to go to their county jail—for an hour—and see its conditions. So long as no one enters a jail except under compulsion, there is very little likelihood of improvement, which must be preceded by public interest.

Mary and Charlie never had children of their own, but she was obviously concerned about youngsters. As she expressed it in the *Survey:*

> *Arizona children are very fortunate in their wonderful climate which makes an outdoor life possible all the year, and in their almost limitless room for play. However, it is to be remembered that every community in the United States was once small enough to afford open space for its children's development, and many of these communities found out later that their rapid growth had wiped out the vacant lot play-space, and that it had to be replaced at great expense. . . . The women of each community could do nothing more useful than interesting themselves in the lives and problems of the children who come before the juvenile court.*

That same year, when Mary was forty, the couple grew tired of city life and bought the Old Camp Rucker Ranch deep in the Chiricahua Mountains. The ranch house was the old adobe fort used in the campaigns against Geronimo's Apaches in the 1880s. It was nestled among junipers and surrounded by rocky peaks, some close to 10,000 feet. Several years later, the fort burned, forcing the Raks to move to a bunkhouse so small that Charlie said one "couldn't cuss the cat without getting fur in your mouth."

Although at first she knew nothing about cattle ("Moreover, I was terrified when the mildest cow even looked my way"), Mary watched and learned. Within a few years she was as competent at managing the livestock as Charlie, and even had her own brand because their second ranch was in her name.

Not all men regarded business-savvy females as favorably as her husband. Like most women in cow country during those days, when someone came by to talk ranching, Mary retreated to the background and left the men to their conversation. But often Charlie was away for long periods, leaving her to run the enterprise. Occasionally, she needed to transact a sale or business deal—provided "the man would allow me to do so."

> *Sometimes, after handling some unimportant business matter with a man during Charlie's temporary absence, I go to the mirror and scan my countenance anxiously, wondering if I really look as foolish and incompetent as these men seem to think me. On the ranch is an unfortunate cow who has been named*

Ballasa, because of a bullet which a careless hunter once sent through her lower jaw. Her mouth is always hanging open; she drools; she looks almost as foolish as the deer-hunter who shot her. After an encounter with some man who assumes that I am incapable of the simplest business transaction, I even fancy I must resemble that poor cow.

Mary spent many hours on horseback, searching for unbranded calves or retrieving heifers for extra feeding. She helped brand, medicate, and vaccinate the cows, and was out almost daily searching for broken fences, monitoring wolf traps, separating out animals bound for sale, checking watering spots, or performing any other of the myriad tasks required by ranchers. Working cattle involves much more than sitting on a well-trained horse. As she once described it: "After a day riding up and down our rocky mountainsides and through oak thickets after cattle, I am convinced the cattle are really working us."

Yet, as tiring as the outside work was, Mary never minded. She loved the sunsets, the sudden downpours, the vaqueros, the spectacular mountain pinnacles surrounding the Rucker basin, and the company of horses and dogs.

"It is not all 'beer and skittles' anywhere," she wrote her New York City friend Gertrude Hills in August 1934, "but I would rather take my hardships in the open. And I know, for I spent three years in a schoolroom and eleven in an office before coming here."

On top of her outdoor chores, Mary's responsibilities also included baking bread, churning butter, putting up preserves, and cooking meals for however many visitors and hired hands were at the ranch that week. Although it was far from her favorite task, she also cleaned the house, giving it "a lick and a promise"—no easy job in a dusty climate without modern conveniences.

However, what's most remarkable about Mary Rak is not her achievement as a ranch woman, but as a writer. Somehow, between keeping house and riding the range, she found time to maintain a lively correspondence—and to write several books and a couple of plays. Each week she resolved to write a thousand words, but finding the time was always a challenge. Many a woman writer can share these sentiments:

Really my chief problem is to get time to write. I am so infernally bogged down by housekeeping and other jobs and never, never can I count absolutely upon an uninterrupted hour. I cook, clean, wash,

mend,—do housekeeping without many conveniences—boss the men when Charlie is away and there is no one to see that I have any time free from interruptions. . . . There is a cave up the canyon. Sometime I'll evict the mountain lioness and her cubs and move in. Her reputation will serve me well.

Mary's first book, *A Social Survey of Arizona*, came out in 1921. *A Cowman's Wife* and *Mountain Cattle* were collections of essays about ranch life and were published in 1934 and 1936 by Houghton Mifflin, and 15,000 words of the latter appeared in *Cosmopolitan* magazine in 1936.

"My endeavor is to write of our own day in a manner that will interest our contemporaries, and at the same time so truthfully that the books may have an historical value if they survive," she told the *Arizona Daily Star* in 1938.

That same year *Border Patrol* was published, and *They Guard the Gates* appeared in 1941. By then, Mary felt she'd used up the ranch material and was ready for something different. She wrote in a September 21, 1941, letter to her friend, Bobbie Scott:

I am recovering from having written a book. The worst stage of the whole business is waiting anywhere from one month to three for a report from a publisher. If the first one decides it is no good then I'll send it off again and wait another spell. Just because I had to have a change and saw no other way to get it, I wrote a mystery. It was hot and dry and whenever I felt mad I hauled off and shot one of my characters. Just barely had left enough to wind up the book, all villains being killed or on their way to jail by chapter 31. If I ever write another, I shall start with more characters so I can kill more and not peter out.

In April 1936 Charlie came down with a combination of flu, pneumonia, and jaundice. He refused to go to the hospital and then became too ill to be moved into town. That same year, Mary was felled by the flu three times in several months. By that time the Raks owned two ranches, Old Camp Rucker in the Chiricahuas and a smaller ranch, Hell's Hip Pocket Ranch, 30 miles away.

Much as they loved the Rucker ranch, the couple reluctantly resolved to sell it. Two ranches 30 miles apart was too much work and too much duplication of effort. The war intervened, but finally Mrs. W. S. (Ella) Dana of New York City bought the property in 1943. She was a wealthy woman who owned another ranch in Nevada, in addition to her Long Island residence.

Mary seems to have had mixed feelings about the sale. Although she was relieved, she described Mrs. Dana as someone "who needs a ranch no more than a cat needs a fig." (Mrs. Dana turned the ranch over to the USDA Forest Service in 1970.)

Moving and getting settled into the smaller ranch took longer than Mary had anticipated. She sounded discouraged in a letter to Gertrude Hills: "Of course I am not writing at present, and that is small loss to anyone since I have three unsold books on hand, which I do not expect to sell during the war, if ever."

Six years later, in 1949, a stroke left Mary unable to write. She died in a Douglas hospital on January 25, 1958, and her ashes were scattered over her ranch.

Thirteen days later, Charlie died. But Mary and her husband live on: The entire Rak estate was left to the University of Arizona for the Mary Kidder Rak scholarship fund for students in agriculture and home economics. All of her papers, including the original manuscripts of the unpublished *Mystery at Pecos High Bridge, The Dark Brown Mystery,* and *At the Crossroads of Life* are still available for perusal at

the Special Collections section of the University of Arizona library.

Most of all, her ranch books are a legacy that continues to show how one woman took on life in the West and made it her own. A literary friend of the family wrote after Mary's death: "Of all the books which attempt to tell about life on a modern cattle ranch, these two [*A Cowman's Wife* and *Mountain Cattle*] seem to me to be the truest and the best."

BIBLIOGRAPHY

JO MONAGHAN

Adams, Mildretta. *Historic Silver City: The Story of the Owyhees.* Homedale, Ida.: Owyhee Chronicle, 1960.

"Cowboy Jo—Was a Woman!" *American-Journal-Examiner,* March 1904.

"Desperate Women: 'Little Jo' Monoghan." *New York Post,* Sunday, 21 December 1952.

"Fifty Years Ago." *The Idaho Statesman,* 24 January 1954.

"Joe Monaghan's Life." *The Idaho Daily Statesman,* 13 January 1904.

"Joe Monaghan Was a Woman." *The Idaho Daily Statesman,* 12 January 1904.

"'Joe' Monnaghan." *Idaho Capital News,* 28 January 1904.

"Local." *Owyhee Avalanche,* 15 January 1904.

Penson, Betty. "Death Ended Cowboy's Masquerade." *The Idaho Statesman,* 17 December 1978.

———. "Little Joe, Idaho Cowboy With a Secret." *The Idaho Statesman,* 4 February 1979.

Rickert, Roger. "Little Jo." *Frontier Time,* June–July (1971): 39, 52–53.

"Was She a Bender." *Lewiston Morning Tribune,* 8 March 1904.

KITTY C. WILKINS

Beal, Merrill D., Ph.D. and Merle W. Wells, Ph.D. *History of Idaho*. Vol. II. New York: Lewis Historical Publishing Company, Inc., 1959.

"Death Takes Colorful Pioneer Horsewoman." *The Idaho Statesman*, 11 October 1936.

Farner, Tom. "The Queen of Diamonds." *Western Horseman*, September (1992): 26–33.

Hart, Arthur A. "Idaho Yesterdays: Horse Queen of Idaho Reaped Much Publicity." *The Idaho Statesman*, 18 December 1972.

"Horses Are Her Delight." *Sioux City Journal*, 26 June 1891.

"Horse Queen of the West." *St. Louis Post–Dispatch*, 10 October 1895.

"Kitty Wilkins 'Horse Queen' Dies Suddenly." *The Idaho Statesman*, 9 October 1936

"Kitty Wilkins Tells Story of Lost Gold Mine Near Jarbidge." *The Idaho Statesman*, 10 January 1926.

"Parents of Idaho's Horse Queen Came West in 1853." *The Idaho Statesman*, 22 April 1928.

"Pioneer Stockman Called By Death." *The Idaho Statesman*, 24 September 1936.

St. John, Harvey. "The Golden Queen." *True West*, July–August (1964): 34–35, 64.

"Their Parents Visit Old Fort Boise in '53." *The Idaho Statesman,* 9 September 1934.

"Twenty Years Ago: The 'Horse Queen of Idaho.'" *The Idaho Statesman,* 18 December 1927.

ALICE DAY PRATT

"Alice Day Pratt," in *The History of Crook County, Oregon.* Prineville: Crook County Historical Society, 1981.

Pratt, Alice Day. *A Homesteader's Portfolio,* with introduction by Molly Glass. Corvallis: Oregon State University Press, 1993. Originally published in 1922.

———. *Three Frontiers.* New York: Vantage Press, 1955.

Raban, Jonathan. *Bad Land: An American Romance.* New York: Pantheon, 1996.

SARAH BOWMAN

Anderson, Greta. "The Great Western." *True West Magazine* (April 2001): 25–26.

Bee, Marge. "Sarah Bowman: The Bell of the U.S. Army." *American Western Magazine* (February 2001). Online: www.readthewest.com.

Christensen, Carol and Tom. *The U.S.–Mexican War.* Miami Lakes, Fla.: Bay Books, 1998.

Elliott, J. F. "The Great Western: Sarah Bowman, Mother and Mistress to the U.S. Army." Journal of Arizona History 30 (Spring 1989): 1–26.

Miller, Ronald Dean. *Shady Ladies of the West.* Los Angeles: Westernlore, 1964.

Sandwich, Brian. *The Great Western: Legendary Lady of the Southwest.* El Paso: Texas Western Press, 1990.

MARY ANN "MOLLY" DYER GOODNIGHT

Crawford, Ann Fears, and Crystal Sasse Ragsdale. *Women in Texas.* Barnett, Tex.: Eakin Press, 1982.

Haley, J. Evetts. *Charles Goodnight: Cowman and Plainsman.* Norman: University of Oklahoma Press, 1949.

Hamner, Laura V. *Short Grass and Longhorns.* Norman: University of Oklahoma Press, 1943.

O'Rear, Sybil J. *Charles Goodnight: Pioneer Cowman.* Austin: Eakin Press, 1990.

Robertson, Pauline Durett and R. L. *Panhandle Pilgrimage.* Amarillo: Paramount Publishing Co., 1978.

Rogers, Mary Beth. *We Can Fly: Stories of Katherine Stinson and Other Gutsy Texas Women.* Austin: Ellen C. Temple, Publisher, 1983.

Warner, Phoebe Kerrick. "The Wife of a Pioneer Ranchman." *The Cattleman* 7 (March 1921): 65–71.

Bibliography

MARY LOUISE CECILIA "TEXAS" GUINAN

Berliner, Louise. *Texas Guinan: Queen of the Nightclubs.* Austin: University of Texas Press, 1993

ANN BASSETT AND JOSIE BASSETT

"Josie Bassett Morris." Pamphlet published by Dinosaur National Monument, Dinosaur, CO, 1989.

Leckenby, Charles H. *The Tread of Pioneers.* Steamboat Springs, CO: Pilot Press, 1944.

Mancini, Richard. *American Legends of the Wild West.* Philadelpia, PA: Courage Books, 1992.

McClure, Grace. *The Bassett Women.* Athens: Ohio University Press/Swallow Press, 1985.

Patterson, Richard. *Butch Cassidy, a Biography.* Lincoln: University of Nebraska Press, 1998.

Ubbelohde, Carl, Maxine Benson, and Duane Smith. *A Colorado History.* Boulder, CO: Pruett Publishing, 1972.

Willis, Ann Bassett. "Queen Ann of Brown's Park." *Colorado Magazine,* April 1952, 81–98; July 1952, 218–235; October 1952, 284–298; and January 1953, 58–76.

Wommack, Linda. *From the Grave: A Roadside Guide to Colorado's Pioneer Cemeteries.* Caldwell, ID: Caxton Press, 1998.

Zwinger, Ann. *Run, River, Run.* New York: Harper & Row, 1975.

FANNIE SPERRY STEELE

Blakely, Reba Perry. "Wild West Shows, Rodeos and No Tears," *World of Rodeo and Western Heritage* (October 1981).

Clark, H. McDonald. "Women's Ex-Rodeo Champ Still Active at 67: Fannie Sperry Steele Operates Ranch in Blackfoot Valley," *Great Falls Tribune*, January 9, 1955.

Clark, Helen. "Fannie Sperry Steele Was a Rodeo Queen 50 Years Too Early," *Montana Farmer-Stockman,* January 21, 1965.

_____."Grand Old Lady of Rodeo: Fanny Sperry Steele," *Western Horseman* (September 1959).

_____. "Montana's Lady Rider," *Inland Empire Magazine of Spokesman–Review,* January 25, 1959.

Henry, Olive. "Fanny Sperry Steele Lives Alone with Her Memories," *Independent Record,* December 10, 1961.

"Horsewoman Steele Dead at 95," *Great Falls Tribune,* February 12, 1983.

Marvine, Dee. "Fannie Sperry Wowed 'Em at First Calgary Stampede," *American West* (August 1987).

Steele, Fannie Sperry. "A Horse Beneath Me . . . Sometimes," *True West* (January/February 1976).

Stiffler, Liz, and Tona Blake. "Fannie Sperry-Steele: Montana's Champion Bronc Rider," *Montana, the Magazine of Western History* (Spring 1982).

NANCY COOPER RUSSELL

Dippie, Brian W., ed. *"Paper Talk": Charlie Russell's American West.* New York: Alfred A. Knopf, in association with the Amon Carter Museum of Western Art, 1979.

McCracken, Harold. *The Charles M. Russell Book.* Garden City, N.J.: Doubleday & Co., 1957.

"Mrs. Russell, Widow of Cowboy Artist, Passes in California," *Great Falls Tribune,* May 25, 1940.

Renner, Ginger K. "Charlie and the Ladies in His Life," *Montana, the Magazine of Western History* (Summer 1984).

Russell, Austin. *Charlie Russell, Cowboy Artist.* New York: Twayne Publishers, 1957.

Russell-Cooper marriage announcement, *Great Falls Tribune,* September 9, 1896.

Russell, Nancy C., ed. *Good Medicine: The Illustrated Letters of Charles M. Russell.* Garden City, N.J.: Doubleday & Co., 1929.

Stauffer, Joan. *Behind Every Man: The Story of Nancy Cooper Russell.* Tulsa, Okla.: Daljo Publishing, 1990.

LAURA GILPIN

Gilpin, Laura. *The Enduring Navaho.* Austin: University of Texas Press, 1968.

———. *The Pueblos: A Camera Chronicle.* New York: Hastings, 1942.

———. *The Rio Grande: River of Destiny.* New York: Duell, Sloan and Pearce, 1949.

Sandweiss, Martha A. *Laura Gilpin: An Enduring Grace.* Fort Worth, Tex.: Amon Carter, 1986.

———. "Laura Gilpin and the Tradition of American Landscape Photography."

PEARL HART

Coleman, Jane Candia. Telephone interview, April 8, 2002.

Editorial. *Arizona Sentinel,* November 25, 1899.

Edwards, Harold L. "Inventing Pearl Hart." *Quarterly of the National Association for Outlaw and Lawman History,* April–June 2002, 30–37.

Hart, Pearl. "An Arizona Episode." *Cosmopolitan,* October 1899, 673–677.

Prison Records, Arizona Territorial Prison State Park, Yuma, Arizona Library. Records of Prisoner No. 1558 (Joe Boot) and No. 1559 (Pearl Hart).

Sortore, Nancy. "Pearl Hart: An End to the Story." *Arizona Daily Star,* September 22, 1974, E1.

MARY KIDDER RAK

"Mary K. Rak's Book Accepted." *Arizona Daily Star,* April 17, 1938.

Rak, Mary Kidder. *A Cowman's Wife.* 1934. Reprint with an introduction by Sandra L. Myres, Austin: The Texas State Historical Association, 1993.

———. *Mountain Cattle.* Boston: Houghton Mifflin Company, 1936.

Rak, Mary (Kidder) Papers. Special Collections, University of Arizona, Tucson.

A Social Survey of Arizona. University of Arizona, University Extension Series, no. 10.

Sonnichsen, C. L. *Cowboys and Cattle Kings: Life on the Range Today.* Norman: University of Oklahoma Press, 1950.